中英双语版

乐尽天真

惊艳千年的苏轼诗词

许渊冲 译
刘小川 评

SELECTED
POEMS
OF
SUSHI

北京联合出版公司

图书在版编目（CIP）数据

乐尽天真：惊艳千年的苏轼诗词 / 许渊冲译；刘小川评. -- 北京：北京联合出版公司，2025.8.
ISBN 978-7-5596-8470-7

Ⅰ. I207.227.442

中国国家版本馆CIP数据核字第2025RD9820号

乐尽天真：惊艳千年的苏轼诗词

译　　者：许渊冲
评　　者：刘小川
出 品 人：赵红仕
责任编辑：肖　桓
封面设计：吴黛君

北京联合出版公司出版
（北京市西城区德外大街83号楼9层 100088）
北京新华先锋出版科技有限公司发行
三河市兴博印务有限公司印刷　新华书店经销
字数194千字　787毫米×1092毫米　1/32　10.5印张
2025年8月第1版　2025年8月第1次印刷
ISBN 978-7-5596-8470-7
定价：49.00元

版权所有，侵权必究
未经书面许可，不得以任何方式转载、复制、翻印本书部分或全部内容。
本书若有质量问题，请与本社图书销售中心联系调换。电话：（010）88876681-8026

目录

凤翔　人生到处知何似

辛丑十一月十九日，既与子由别于郑州西门之外，马上赋诗一篇寄之	002
和子由渑池怀旧	006
和子由踏青	008
十二月十四日夜微雪，明日早往南溪小酌至晚	012
别岁	014
守岁	018
春夜	022
石鼻城	024

杭州　淡妆浓抹总相宜

戏子由	028

除夜直都厅，囚系皆满，日暮不得返舍，
　　因题一诗于壁　　　　　　　　　032
虞姬墓　　　　　　　　　　　　　　034
游金山寺　　　　　　　　　　　　　036
自金山放船至焦山　　　　　　　　　040
雨中游天竺灵感观音院　　　　　　　044
有美堂暴雨　　　　　　　　　　　　046
六月二十七日望湖楼醉书（五首选三）048
饮湖上初晴后雨（二首选一）　　　　052
新城道中（二首选一）　　　　　　　054
望海楼晚景（五首选三）　　　　　　056
八月十五日看潮五绝　　　　　　　　060
催试官考较戏作　　　　　　　　　　064
法惠寺横翠阁　　　　　　　　　　　068
冬至日独游吉祥寺　　　　　　　　　072
书双竹湛师房（二首选一）　　　　　074
吴中田妇叹　　　　　　　　　　　　076
於潜女　　　　　　　　　　　　　　080
行香子·过七里濑　　　　　　　　　082
行香子·丹阳寄述古　　　　　　　　086
行香子·述怀　　　　　　　　　　　090
醉落魄·离京口作　　　　　　　　　094

醉落魄·苏州阊门留别	096
南乡子·送述古	098
南乡子·梅花词和杨元素	100
江城子·湖上与张先同赋	102
昭君怨·送别	106
瑞鹧鸪·观潮	108
虞美人·有美堂赠述古	110
少年游·润州作,代人寄远	112
腊日游孤山访惠勤惠思二僧	114
江城子·孤山竹阁送述古	118

密州　老夫聊发少年狂

沁园春·赴密州,早行,马上寄子由	124
江城子·密州出猎	128
蝶恋花·密州上元	132
水调歌头(明月几时有)	134
江城子·乙卯正月二十日夜记梦	138
更漏子·送孙巨源	142
永遇乐·寄孙巨源	144

徐州　问言豆叶几时黄

阳关曲·中秋作	150
浣溪沙·徐门石潭谢雨，道上作五首	152
浣溪沙（山色横侵蘸晕霞）	160
浣溪沙（风压轻云贴水飞）	162
浣溪沙·咏橘	164
永遇乐（明月如霜）	166
续丽人行	170
除夜大雪，留潍州，元日早晴，	
遂行，中途雪复作	174
李思训画长江绝岛图	178
百步洪（二首选一）	182
舟中夜起	186
陈季常所蓄朱陈村嫁娶图二首	188

湖州　小园幽榭枕苹汀

南歌子·湖州作	192
端午遍游诸寺得禅字	194

黄州　世事一场大梦

雨晴后，步至四望亭下渔池上，遂自乾明寺前东冈上归二首	200
西江月·黄州中秋	204
西江月（照野㳽㳽浅浪）	206
定风波（莫听穿林打叶声）	208
浣溪沙（山下兰芽短浸溪）	212
念奴娇·赤壁怀古	214
临江仙·夜归临皋	218
卜算子·黄州定慧院寓居作	220
南乡子·重九涵辉楼呈徐君猷	222
鹧鸪天（林断山明竹隐墙）	224
满庭芳（三十三年）	226
满庭芳（蜗角虚名）	230
满庭芳·留别雪堂	234
虞美人（波声拍枕长淮晓）	238
调笑令（渔父）	240
洞仙歌（冰肌玉骨）	242
洞仙歌·咏柳	246
红梅（三首选一）	248

正月二十日与潘、郭二生出郊寻春，忽记
　　去年是日同至女王城作诗，乃和前韵　　250
春日　　252
寒食雨二首　　254
次荆公韵　　258
题西林壁　　260
琴诗　　262
南堂（五首选二）　　264
海棠　　266
归宜兴留题竹西寺　　268
惠崇春江晚景二首　　270
南乡子·集句　　272

京都　一朵红云捧玉皇

水龙吟·次韵章质夫杨花词　　276
贺新郎（乳燕飞华屋）　　280
鹊桥仙·七夕送陈令举　　284
八声甘州·寄参寥子　　286
临江仙·送钱穆父　　290
书李世南所画秋景（二首选一）　　292
书鄢陵王主簿所画折枝二首　　294

赠刘景文 298
上元侍饮楼上三首呈同列（三首选一） 300

儋州　此生归路愈茫然

慈湖夹阻风（五首选三） 304
纵笔 308
被酒独行，遍至子云、威、徽、
　　先觉四黎之舍（三首选二） 310
纵笔（三首选一） 312
澄迈驿通潮阁二首 314
过岭 316
归朝欢·和苏坚伯固 318
蝶恋花·春景 322
西江月·梅花 324

辛丑十一月十九日，既与子由①别于郑州西门之外，马上赋诗一篇寄之

不饮胡为醉兀兀②？
此心已逐归鞍③发。
归人犹自念庭闱④，
今我何以慰寂寞？
登高回首坡垅⑤隔，
惟见乌帽出复没。
苦寒念尔衣裘薄，
独骑瘦马踏残月。
路人行歌⑥居人乐，
童仆怪我苦凄恻。
亦知人生要有别，
但恐岁月去飘忽。

① 子由：苏轼弟苏辙，字子由。
② 兀兀：昏沉的样子。
③ 归鞍：回家所乘坐的马。
④ 庭闱：指父母的住所。
⑤ 坡垅：丘陵。
⑥ 行歌：边走边唱。

苏轼第一次与子由远别去凤翔赴任，心中不由得生出万般不舍，以至达到了神思恍惚的境地。站在高处眺望子由回京的身影，心已随子由一同离去，只看见子由的乌帽忽隐忽现。又担心子由衣裳太薄，残月下独自骑着瘦马归去分外孤单，而自己呢，也一脸凄凉忧伤。才刚别离，却又想着他日

A Poem to My Brother Ziyou, Composed on Horseback after Parting with Him at the Western Gate of the Capital on the 19th Day of the 11th Lunar Month

Why do I look so drunken without drinking wine?
My heart is going back with your home-going steed.
Your thoughts turn to our parents and ancestral shrine.
How can I be consoled with the lonely life I'll lead?
Ascending a height, I look back and feel so sad
To see your black cap now appear, now disappear.
It is now biting cold and you are thinly clad,
Riding a lean nag 'neath the waning moon so drear.
Wayfarers sing abroad, people are glad at home,
My houseboy wonders why alone I'm desolate.
I know people may meet or part, settle down or roam,
But I dread to think how quickly years evaporate.

夜雨对床，共听窗外萧萧雨声。此诗写离愁别恨，有依依不舍，亦有对他日（未来）的希冀，道出了兄弟情深，读之，令人怦然动容，沉浸其中。

寒灯相对记畴昔⑦,
夜雨何时听萧瑟⑧?
君知此意不可忘,
慎勿苦爱高官职!

⑦畴昔:往日。
⑧夜雨句:苏轼自注:"尝有夜雨对床之言,故云尔。"

Facing a cold lamp, I relive the bygone days.

When may we listen to bleak wind on rainy night?

You know what I mean and must bear in mind always:

Don't outstay your office of which you should make light.

和子由渑池①怀旧

人生到处知何似?
应似飞鸿踏雪泥。
泥上偶然留指爪,
鸿飞那复计东西!
老僧②已死成新塔,
坏壁③无由见旧题。
往日崎岖还记否?
路长人困蹇驴④嘶。

①渑(miǎn)池:今河南省渑池县。
②老僧:僧人奉闲。
③坏壁:奉闲的僧舍。
④蹇(jiǎn)驴:跛脚的驴子。

"雪泥鸿爪"乃空幻无常之禅语耶?非也!人生所过,皆偶然而已,飞鸿不执着于指爪旧迹,转瞬即追寻更广阔的天地。老僧已去,题壁也无,往日行路崎岖这样深刻的记忆却不曾消散。旧迹不可恋,记忆不可失,但人生需要更广阔的天空!果如其言,个体若飞鸿渺小的苏轼,其生命的维度超越了时空。

然此诗亦一语成谶,苏轼一生路长人困、一生崎岖,苏辙亦言其"涉世多艰……如鸿风飞"!诗成于仕途之始,却似写于仕途之终!

Recalling the Old Days at Mianchi in the Same Rhymes as Ziyou's Poem

What do you think is human life like here or there?
It seems like a swan's traces on mud or on snow.
See the claw and nail prints by chance mud and snow bear.
Will the flying swan care what it has left below?
The old monk, dead, has left but a dagoba new;
The verse we wrote was gone with the wall in decay.
What I remember of the journey made with you
Is a weary long way and the lame donkey's bray.

和①子由踏青

东风②陌上惊微尘,
游人初乐岁华新③。
人闲正好路旁饮,
麦短未怕游车轮。
城中居人厌城郭,
喧阗④晓出空四邻。
歌鼓惊山草木动,
箪瓢⑤散野乌鸢⑥驯。
何人聚众称道人?
遮道卖符色怒嗔⑦。
宜蚕使汝茧如瓮,
宜畜使汝羊如麇⑧。

①和:唱和。
②东风:春风。
③岁华新:新年伊始。
④喧阗(tián):喧嚣吵闹。
⑤箪(dān)瓢:盛饭的箪和盛酒水的瓢,借指饭食。
⑥乌鸢(yuān):老鹰类属的飞禽。
⑦色怒嗔:面带怒色。
⑧麇(jūn):獐子。

　　这首诗写家乡眉山岁首乡俗,回忆青少年时在家乡新春之际,与家人及"城中居人"游春踏青的盛况,具有浓郁的乡情。诗中刻画了一位卖符道人的生动形象,丰富了诗歌的内容,增添了诗歌的情趣和郊游的喜庆气氛。全诗语言浅显,情真意切,耐人寻味。

Rhyming with Ziyou's "Treading the Green"

The east wind raises a fine dust on the pathways,
Excursionists are glad to enjoy new year's pleasure.
People may drink by the roadside as they have leisure,
Short wheat are not afraid of the wheels of the chaise.
Townsfolk are tired of living within city wall,
They make much noise on leaving their house in the morn.
Songs and drums jar the hills and shake trees, grass and thorn;
Picnic baskets invite tame birds, crows, kites and all.
Who is there drawing round a crowd, barring the ways?
It is a Taoist priest who sells his charms and says:
"Buy my charms and your cocoon will sure grow as big
As a jar and your sheep as a pig."

路人未必信此语,
强为买服禳⁹新春。
道人得钱径沽酒,
醉倒自谓吾符神!

⑨禳(ráng):祈福消灾。

Passers-by may not believe in his words so fine,

They buy charms anyway to consecrate the spring.

The priest gets money and goes to a shop of wine,

Drunken, he boasts his charms are wonder-working thing.

十二月十四日夜微雪，明日早往南溪小酌至晚

南溪得雪真无价，
走马来看及^①未消。
独自披榛寻履迹，
最先犯晓^②过朱桥。
谁怜屋破眠无处？
坐觉村饥语不嚣。
惟有暮鸦知客意，
惊飞千片落寒条。

①及：赶上，趁着。
②犯晓：打破清晨的寂静。

这首诗描写自己在寒冷的冬日，一大早就迫不及待地骑着马出门探雪，独自穿越落雪纷纷的丛林，得以在天明时最早通过朱桥，第一个看到了雪原美景。接着笔锋一转，写贫苦的百姓在天寒地冻时该如何生活，又有谁来怜悯他们，他的心境也不由得变得凄凉起来。整首诗也因颈联的点睛之笔，远离了纯粹的"风花雪月"，使诗意变得更深邃，更温暖动人。

It Snowed on the Night of the 14th Day of the 12th Lunar Month. I Went to the Southern Valley on the Next Morning and Drank There Till Dusk

The snow in Southern Valley is priceless indeed,

I come there on horseback before it melts away.

Alone, I follow the trail in a cloak of reed,

First to cross the ochre bridge at the break of day.

Who pities the homeless who have nowhere to sleep?

I find villagers hungry whose voices are low.

Only the crows at dusk know why I'm thinking deep,

Startled, they fly and shed a thousand flakes of snow.

别岁

故人适^①千里,
临别尚迟迟。
人行犹可复,
岁行那可追。
问岁安所之?
远在天一涯。
已逐东流水,
赴海归无时。
东邻酒初熟,
西舍彘^②亦肥。
且为一日欢,
慰此穷年悲。

①适:往。
②彘(zhì):猪。

这首诗是苏轼在宋仁宗嘉祐七年(1062)的辞岁诗,以白描的手法,写出了古代蜀地酒肉相邀的"别岁"风俗。岁月流逝无法追回,就像东流水奔入大海再也无法回转。东邻煮好了酒,西邻做好了肥猪肉,那就高兴地喝酒吧,聊以告

Farewell to the Old Year

When an old friend is to go far away,

Long, long will he linger before he parts.

Though gone away, he may come back some day.

Where can we find the old year once it departs?

May I ask whither the old year has passed?

At the end of the earth it leaves no track.

It is gone with the water flowing fast

To the East Sea and will never come back.

Wine is warmed by our neighbors on the east

And the pork of those on the west is fat.

I'd like to have one happy day at least

So that the lean year may not be grieved at.

慰这即将逝去的时光。不要一味感叹岁月的无情,否则新的一年也即将流逝;不要总是回顾往昔,岁月留下的只有衰老。蜀之风俗如是。

勿嗟旧岁别,
行与新岁辞。
去去勿回顾,
还君老与衰。

Do not sigh for the departing old year!

Soon we shall say goodbye to New Year's Day.

Do not look back but let them disappear.

Man will grow old and his powers decay.

守岁

欲知垂尽①岁,
有似赴壑②蛇。
修鳞③半已没,
去意谁能遮?
况欲系其尾,
虽勤知奈何!
儿童强④不睡,
相守夜讙哗⑤。
晨鸡且勿唱,
更鼓畏添挝⑥。
坐久灯烬落,
起看北斗斜。

①垂尽:即将结束。
②壑:山谷。
③修鳞:指长蛇的躯体。
④强(qiǎng):勉强。
⑤讙哗:喧哗。
⑥挝(zhuā):敲打,此处指更鼓声。

这首诗用比喻写时光飞逝,就像钻进洞穴里的蛇,长长的身子已经钻进去一大半了,没人能够阻拦,就像你想要抓住蛇的尾巴,动作再快也不可能。接着,写孩子们都不肯去睡觉,聚在一起尽情玩乐,不愿听到夜晚的更鼓声和晨鸡打鸣,直到灯烛的灰烬落下,起身看见北斗星斜挂空中。最后,抒发对旧年将去的不舍。

Staying up All Night on New Year's Eve

The end of the year is drawing near

As a snake crawls back to its hole.

We see half its body disappear

And soon we'll lose sight of the whole.

If we try to tie down its tail,

We can't succeed whate'er we do.

Children will stay up and regale

Themselves with feast the whole night through.

Cocks, wake not the dawn with your song;

Drums, do not boom out the hour now!

The wick is burned as I sit long,

I rise to see the slanting Plough.

明年岂无年,
心事恐蹉跎。
努力尽今夕,
少年犹可夸。

Will there be no New Year's Eve next year?

I am afraid time waits for none.

Let us enjoy tonight with cheer

So that childhood will longer run.

春夜

春宵一刻①值千金,
花有清香月有阴②。
歌管③楼台声细细,
秋千院落夜沉沉。

①一刻:比喻时间短暂。刻,计时单位。
②月有阴:指月光在花下投射出朦胧的阴影。
③歌管:歌声和管乐声。

　　这首诗紧扣"春夜"来写,描写了花的清香、月光的朦胧阴影、楼台的歌声和管乐声,还有秋千院落,等等。视觉、嗅觉、听觉,多感官联动,将春夜的美好悉数呈现,让人深受感染,置身其中。

Spring Night

A moment of spring night is worth its length of gold,
When flowers spread on moonlight and shade fragrance cold.
The slender flute from the bower plays music slender;
The tender night on garden swing casts shadow tender.

石鼻城[1]

平时战国今无在，
陌上征夫自不闲。
北客初来试新险，
蜀人从此送残山。
独穿暗月朦胧里，
愁渡奔河苍茫间。
渐入西南风景变，
道旁修竹水潺潺。

[1] 石鼻城：即武城镇，位于宝鸡东北，相传为诸葛亮所建，曾是蜀、魏的战场。

石鼻城地理位置特殊，靠近南北地域分界线。南来北往的人，路过这个地方，所见皆同，感触却各异。诗人便从这"异"字入手，从古今变迁、旅人感受、景观变化描绘石鼻城，似写城更似说理，引发读者对历史、自然和生活变化的深刻思考。

The Stone-nose Town

Where are the belligerent states of bygone days?
Wayfarers are trudging on their way without cheer.
New-come Northerners on the peril fix their gaze;
The mountaineers part with their last steep mountain here.
Alone, I make my way dimly lit by moonlight;
Saddened, I cross the river shrouded in the haze.
The Southwest land affords a quite different sight:
The ripples whisper with roadside bamboo they graze.

杭州

淡妆浓抹总相宜

戏子由

宛丘①先生长如丘，
宛丘学舍小如舟。
常时低头诵经史，
忽然欠伸屋打头。
斜风吹帷雨注面，
先生不愧旁人羞。
任从饱死笑方朔，
肯为雨立求秦优②！
眼前勃豀③何足道，
处置六凿④须天游。
读书万卷不读律⑤，
致君尧舜知无术⑥。

① 宛丘：陈州的别称。因为苏辙时任陈州州学教授，故称"宛丘先生"。
② 秦优：指秦始皇的歌童旃。
③ 勃豀（xī）：争吵。
④ 六凿：即喜、怒、哀、乐、爱、恶六情。
⑤ 律：法律。
⑥ 术：治术。

这首诗题为"戏子由"，但其旨不在"戏"而在"赞"子由，赞子由的秉性为人，宁可过清苦的生活也不曲己求人，并自嘲书愤，抒发了自己在政治上受排挤，以及对所鄙视的达官贵人的愤懑之情。全诗运用对比手法，以相反的事，突

Written to Ziyou in Joke

My brother's tall as Confucius is said to be,
But his room in the schoolhouse looks like a boat small.
He bends his head while reading classics and history,
Suddenly he yawns, his head bumps against the wall.
The wind blows screens aside and raindrops into his face,
The onlookers feel sorry but he does not care.
The starving may be jeered at by well-fed men base,
He won't beg for shelter though rain drenches his hair.
He cares not for the discomforts before the eye,
If he can let his six spirits soar in the sky.
He's read ten thousand books without reading the law.
How could he serve a sovereign without a flaw!

出兄弟二人共同的不得志，貌似戏谑却深沉，是用喜剧的手法谱写悲愤之曲，显示了苏诗"嬉笑怒骂，皆成文章"的特色。

劝农⁷冠盖闹如云,
送老齑⁸盐甘似蜜。
门前万事不挂眼,
头虽长低气不屈!
余杭⁹别驾无功劳,
画堂五丈容旂旄⑩。
重楼跨空雨声远,
屋多人少风骚骚。
平生所惭今不耻,
坐对疲氓重鞭箠⑪。
道逢阳虎⑫呼与言,
心知其非口诺唯。
居高志下真何益,
气节消缩今无几。
文章小技安足程,
先生别驾旧齐名。
如今衰老俱无用,
付与时人分重轻!

⑦劝农:指朝廷派遣到各地视察农业情况的官吏。
⑧齑(jī):指腌菜,切碎的酱菜。
⑨余杭:即杭州。苏轼时任杭州通判,故以"余杭别驾"自称。
⑩旂旄(qí máo):牦牛尾于杆首的旌旗,军将所建。
⑪箠:杖刑。
⑫阳虎:即阳货,孔子所鄙视而不愿意与之见面的人。

The inspectors of agriculture come in throng,
Honey-like vegetables are given to the old.
Nothing at the door will remain in his eyes for long,
Though his head oft bends low, his spirit is still bold.
Official of Hangzhou, I've done no worthy deed,
My painted hall is so large that flags can be displayed.
My mansion stands high and from noise of rain is freed,
With rooms uninhabited soughing winds invade.
I'm no longer ashamed of what I used to be,
And punish with flogging the accused before me.
I greet those I dislike when we meet on the way,
Though I know they are wrong, yet I say only "Aye".
What is the use of a high literary fame
When ebbs our moral courage and lowers our aim?
The trifling art of writing is of no avail,
You and I, while young, we attained the same renown.
We become worthless now we're decrepit and frail.
Let our contemporaries play us up or down!

除夜直都厅,囚系皆满,日暮不得返舍,因题一诗于壁

除日当早归,
官事乃见留。
执笔对之泣,
哀此系中囚:
小人营糇粮①,
堕网②不知羞。
我亦恋薄禄,
因循失归休。
不须论贤愚,
均是为食谋。
谁能暂纵遣?
闵默③愧前修④。

①糇(hóu)粮:干粮。
②堕网:堕入法网,即犯法。
③闵默:亦作悯默,心中有忧虑,但说不出来。
④前修:先贤。

苏轼写这首诗时,全国正施行青苗、免役、市易诸法,浙西兼行水利、盐法,杭州许多贫苦的百姓因奔走贩盐触犯了新法,被关在牢中。除夕日原本是万家团圆的日子,可是他们有家不得归,有冤不得伸,有苦无处诉。苏轼认为百姓是为了糊口才触犯法律的,作此诗为被囚系的百姓鸣不平,表达了对民生的关切,对百姓的同情。

Seeing Prisoners on New Year's Eve

I should go back early on New Year's Eve,
But my official duty detains me.
Holding my writing brush in hand, I grieve
For I am like these prisoners I see.
They cannot earn an honest livelihood,
And feel no shame at committing a crime.
I won't resign my office which I should,
And get into a rut and lose my time.
Don't ask who is foolish or who is wise.
All of us alike must scheme for a meal.
Who can be carefree from his fall and rise?
Silent before the sage, what shame I feel!

虞姬墓

帐下佳人拭泪痕,
门前壮士气如云。
仓黄不负君王^①意,
只有虞姬与郑君^②。

①君王：指项羽。
②郑君：即郑荣，西楚忠臣。此处指不负项羽的人。

垓下之战，四面楚歌，霸王歌曰："虞兮虞兮奈若何！"虞姬拭泪和歌："大王意气尽，贱妾何聊生？"帐外八百壮士拼死一战却终究不敌，项羽自刎乌江，虞姬践诺自尽！军阵列列尽皆降敌，唯有郑荣一人坚持避讳霸王之名"籍"，被高祖刘邦驱逐。虞姬与郑荣，一死一生，皆忠贞之人！可见生与死不是忠贞的绝对标准，在其志在其心！

有宋一代，边境群雄环伺，苏公颂虞姬与郑君，意之深也！

Lady Yu's Tomb

In the tent fair ladies wiped away their tears;
At the door brave men gathered like a mass of cloud.
Who justified the king's trust in critical years?
Of Lady Yu and General Zheng he could be proud.

游金山寺①

我家江水初发源,
宦游直送江入海。
闻道潮头一丈高,
天寒尚有沙痕在。
中泠②南畔石盘陀③,
古来出没随涛波。
试登绝顶望乡国,
江南江北青山多。
羁愁畏晚寻归楫④,
山僧苦留看落日。
微风万顷靴文细,
断霞半空鱼尾赤。

①金山寺:在今江苏省镇江市西北的长江边的金山上。宋时位于江心。
②中泠:泉名,位于金山以西。
③石盘陀:形容石头巨大。
④归楫(jí):从金山回去的船。楫原是船桨,此处以部分代替整体。

　　此诗为七言古诗,是苏轼于熙宁四年(1071)赴杭州途中经金山寺夜宿而作,乃宋代山水游览诗中的名篇。起句便出奇,将其万里行程、半生仕宦与长江水奔流入海巧妙结合,一笔道尽眉州、岷江、长江、镇江的地理关系而又饱含人生若流水之意,非东坡不可道。接着描绘登高远眺之景,动静结合、虚实相生,勾起浓浓的思乡之情。

Visiting the Temple of Golden Hill

My native town lies where the River takes its source,
As official I go downstream to the seaside.
'Tis said white-crested waves rise ten feet high at full tide,
On this cold day the sand bears traces of their force.
There stands a massive boulder south of Central Fountain,
Emerging or submerged as the tides fall or rise.
I climb atop to see where my native town lies,
But find by riverside green mountain on green mountain.
Home-sick, I will go back by boat lest I be late,
But the monk begs me to stay and view the setting sun.
The breeze ripples the water and fine webs are spun;
Rosy clouds in mid-air like fish-tails undulate.

是时江月初生魄[5]，
二更月落天深黑。
江心似有炬火明，
飞焰照山栖乌惊。
怅然归卧心莫识，
非鬼非人竟何物？
江山如此不归山，
江神见怪惊我顽。
我谢[6]江神岂得已，
有田不归如江水[7]！

[5]初生魄：新月初生。
[6]谢：告罪，道歉。
[7]如江水：中国古人发誓时常用的誓词，表明发誓人对于誓言的坚定和真诚。

Then the moon on the river sheds her new-born light,
By second watch she sinks into the darkened skies.
From the heart of the river a torch seems to rise,
Its flames light up the mountains and the crows take flight.
Bewildered, I come back and go to bed, lost in thought:
It's not a work of man or ghost. Then what is it?
It must be the River God's warning for me to quit
And go to my home-town, which I can't set at nought.
Thanking the God, I say I'm reluctant to stay,
If I won't go home, like these waves I'll pass away!

自金山放船至焦山[1]

金山楼观何眈眈[2],
撞钟击鼓闻淮南[3]。
焦山何有有修竹,
采薪汲水僧两三。
云霾[4]浪打人迹绝,
时有沙户[5]祈春蚕。
我来金山更留宿,
而此[6]不到心怀惭。
同游兴尽决独往,
赋命[7]穷薄轻江潭。
清晨无风浪自涌,
中流歌啸倚半酣。

①焦山:在长江中,因汉代焦先曾隐居于此,故名。
②眈眈:深邃的样子。
③淮南:指扬州。
④云霾:阴云,形容翻滚的波浪。
⑤沙户:生活在沙洲上的人家。
⑥此:指焦山。
⑦赋命:天生的命运。

此诗为诗人游金山寺后再游焦山所作。开篇即以金山之壮丽衬托焦山之荒僻,再言其云霾浪打少有人迹,而诗人不惧江潭之险独往,自嘲"赋命穷薄"而又"中流歌啸倚半酣",真真是无有所惧,豪气干云。苏辙有《和子瞻焦山》诗可作对读:金山游遍入焦山,舟轻帆急须臾间。涉江已远风浪阔,游人到此皆争还。山头冉冉万竿竹,楼阁不见门长关。

Boating from the Golden Hill to the Hermit's Hill

How gaudy does the Temple of Golden Hill glare!
To Huainan spread its beating drum and ringing bell.
What has the Hermit's Hill but bamboo here and there
And two or three monks drawing water from the well?
On its deserted shore veiled in dim mist waves beat,
Only to seek silk-worms in spring will peasants come.
In Golden Hill I stayed o'ernight to rest my feet.
Without seeing Hermit's Hill, how sorry I'd become!
My companions were disinclined to come with me.
Disfavored man alone of whirlpool risk make light.
Waves surge although the morning of the wind is free,
Half drunken, I sing in mid-stream with sweet delight.

老僧下山惊客至，
迎笑喜作巴人谈。
自言久客忘乡井，
只有弥勒为同龛⁸。
困眠得就纸帐⁹暖，
饱食未厌山蔬甘。
山林饥卧古亦有，
无田不退宁非贪？
展禽⁽¹⁰⁾虽未三见黜⁽¹¹⁾，
叔夜⁽¹²⁾自知七不堪。
行当投劾⁽¹³⁾谢簪组，
为我佳处留茅庵。

⑧同龛（kān）：同室相伴。龛，供佛像的小阁子。
⑨纸帐：纸制的帐子。
⑩展禽：春秋时期鲁国大夫，即柳下惠。
⑪黜（chù）：罢免。
⑫叔夜：即嵇康，字叔夜。
⑬投劾：呈递弹劾自己的状文。古代弃官的一种方式。

The old monk comes downhill, surprised to see a guest,
And glad to greet his compatriot with a smile.
He says he has forgotten his home-town in the west,
Living together with Maitreya on this isle.
He sleeps in a warm paper curtain when tired and cold;
Hungry, he likes to eat mountain vegetables sweet.
The mountaineers have suffered hunger since days old;
Not greedy, the landless should make good their retreat.
Although I have not been dismissed from office thrice,
Yet I know there are seven things I cannot bear.
Soon I will resign for I am not free from vice,
I wish to live in thatched temple free from care.

雨中游天竺灵感观音院[1]

蚕欲老,
麦半黄,
前山后山雨浪浪[2]。
农夫辍耒[3]女废筐,
白衣仙人[4]在高堂。

[1]灵感观音院:位于杭州上天竺,五代时钱镠所建。
[2]浪浪:形容雨声之响。
[3]辍耒(chuò lěi):停止农作。
[4]白衣仙人:即观音菩萨,此处暗讽官吏。

这首诗写正当蚕老、麦黄之际,偏遭淫雨,这对农夫桑女是很沉重的打击。白衣仙人观音菩萨却高坐堂上,无动于衷,漠不关心。表面是责备神像土偶无知,实际是讽刺当政者只知养尊处优,不管百姓死活。全诗语言通俗,状景生动,音节流畅,声韵铿锵,讽刺之意含蓄不露,耐人寻味。

Visiting the Temple of the Compassionate God of Mercy on a Rainy Day

Silkworms grow old,

Wheat turns half gold.

On both sides of the hill the rain is pouring its fill.

Women can't weave baskets nor can men till the ground,

But high in the hall sits the immortal white-gowned.

有美堂[1]暴雨

游人脚底一声雷,
满座顽云[2]拨不开。
天外黑风吹海立,
浙东飞雨过江来。
十分潋滟[3]金樽凸[4],
千杖敲铿[5]羯鼓[6]催。
唤起谪仙泉洒面,
倒倾鲛室[7]泻琼瑰[8]。

[1] 有美堂:位于杭州吴山。
[2] 顽云:浓厚的云。
[3] 潋滟:水波相连的样子。
[4] 凸:高出。
[5] 敲铿(kēng):啄木鸟啄木的声音,此处指打鼓声。
[6] 羯(jié)鼓:一种出自西域的乐器。
[7] 鲛室:神话中海中鲛人的居所,此处指大海。
[8] 琼瑰:珠玉。

脚底惊雷、云聚风呼、天外飞雨倾泻而下,西湖水波有如金樽满溢,雨声铿锵有若千杖敲羯鼓,天地仿佛要用这天外飞泉唤醒谪仙人李太白,激荡出他胸中琼瑰般的锦绣文章!

全诗直抒胸臆豪迈雄阔,写出一场震慑人心的壮观暴雨;想象飞腾而不突兀,直令人拍案叫绝!

Tempest at the Scenic Hall

Sight-seers hear from below a sudden thunder roars;
A skyful of storm-clouds cannot be dissipated.
The dark wind from on high raises a sea agitated;
The flying rain from the east crosses river shores.
Like wine o'erflowing golden cup full to the brim
And thousands of sticks beating the drum of sheepskin.
Heaven pours water on the poet's face and chin
That he might write with dragon's scales and pearls a hymn.

六月二十七日望湖楼醉书（五首选三）

一

黑云翻墨①未遮②山，
白雨跳珠乱入船。
卷地风来忽吹散，
望湖楼下水如天。

①翻墨：打翻的墨水，形容云层很黑。
②遮：遮蔽。
③水枕句：大意是说卧于船中，只见山头上下起伏，而不觉水波摇动。

二

放生鱼鳖逐人来，
无主荷花到处开。
水枕能令山俯仰③，
风船解与月徘徊。

　　这组诗是作者游览西湖，在船上看到奇妙的湖光山色，再到望湖楼眺望湖景时所作。所选第一首尤佳，写夏日西湖上一场来去匆匆的暴雨，在一刹那之间，乌云密布，暴雨骤降，但转眼间又风起云散，望湖楼外，水天一色。诗人对暴风雨前后的景色变化写得十分生动，富有特色。

Written While Drunken in the Lake View Pavilion on the 27th Day of the 6th Lunar Month

I

Like spilt ink dark clouds spread o'er the hills as a pall;
Like bouncing pearls the raindrops in the boat run riot.
A sudden rolling gale comes and dispels them all,
Below Lake View Pavilion sky-mirrored water's quiet.

II

Captive fish and turtles set free swim after men,
Here and there in full bloom are lotuses unowned.
Pillowed on the waves, we see hills rise now, fall then;
Boating in the wind, the moon seems to whirl around.

三

未成小隐④聊中隐⑤,
可得长闲胜暂闲。
我本无家更安往?
故乡无此好湖山。

④小隐:隐居在山林。
⑤中隐:指闲官。

III

Not yet secluded, in official life I seek pleasure;

Free for some time, I long to enjoy longer leisure.

Homeless as I might have been, where may I go then? Where?

The lakes and hills in my home-town are not so fair.

饮湖上^①初晴后雨（二首选一）

水光潋滟晴方好,
山色空蒙^②雨亦奇。
欲把西湖比西子^③,
淡妆浓抹总相宜^④。

①饮湖上：在西湖上泛舟饮酒。
②空蒙：缥缈的样子。
③西子：西施。
④相宜：合适，自然。

西湖得盛名，东坡功占一半！

晴时水光潋滟，雨时山色空蒙，湖山韵致有如西子之美，不论淡妆浓抹、捧心展颜，皆灵动变化、风采卓然！东坡首将西湖与西子联动，从此西子湖永远为杭州代言！

Drinking at the Lake First in Sunny and then in Rainy Weather

The brimming waves delight the eye on sunny days;

The dimming hills give a rare view in rainy haze.

The West Lake looks like the fair lady at her best;

Whether she is richly adorned or plainly dressed.

新城道中（二首选一）

东风知我欲山行，
吹断檐间积雨声。
岭上晴云披絮帽①，
树头初日挂铜钲②。
野桃含笑竹篱短，
溪柳自摇沙水清。
西崦③人家应最乐，
煮芹烧笋饷④春耕。

①絮帽：棉帽。
②钲（zhēng）：古代铜制乐器。
③西崦（yān）：此处泛指山。
④饷：用食物招待别人。

    这首诗以轻快活泼的笔调，抒写自己自富阳赴新城途中的见闻和愉快心情，表现出诗人向往自然、热爱自然的情趣。首联写多情的东风很会察言观色，猜透了诗人心中的忧虑，立即慷慨相助，吹得雨散云开；颔联用比喻写山峰戴上洁白的絮帽，树梢挂着明亮的铜锣，把晴天云朵和初升的太阳写得形象生动而富有神采；颈联用拟人手法写进得山来，桃花

On My Way to New Town

The eastern wind foresees I will go to the wood;
It blows off endless songs sung by rain on the eaves.
The mountain's crowned with rainbow cloud like silken hood;
The rising sun like a brass gong hangs o'er the leaves.
Peach blossoms smile o'er the bamboo fence not tall;
Willow trees by the clear sand-paved brook sway and swing.
Folks in the Western Hills should be happiest of all;
They send well-cooked food to those who till in spring.

笑，柳条舞，这样殷勤好客；尾联一个"应"字，写西山人家怡然自乐的心情及其耕种之乐。新奇的比喻，巧妙的拟人，不仅描绘出山溪花木之美，而且烘托出诗人山行之乐、内心之乐和景色之美。

望海楼①晚景（五首选三）

一

海上涛头一线来，
楼前指顾②雪成堆。
从今潮上君须上，
更看银山二十回。

二

横风吹雨入楼斜，
壮观应须好句夸。
雨过潮平江海碧，
电光时掣紫金蛇③。

① 望海楼：又名望潮楼，位于杭州凤凰山上。
② 指顾：指点顾盼之间，形容时间极短。
③ 紫金蛇：比喻闪电。

这组诗共五首，分别咏江潮、雨电、秋风、江景等，各具情韵。所选第二首尤佳，写在望海楼所见风雨，于写景中蕴含一种人生的哲理。诗开头写风雨的气势很猛，转眼间却是雨阑云散，风停潮息，海阔天晴，变幻之快使人目瞪口呆。其实不只自然界是这样，人世间的事情，往往也是如此变幻莫测。

Evening Views from the Seaside Pavilion

I

The rising tide comes in from the sea in a row,

Below the Pavilion in a twinkling heaps up snow.

From now on you should come with the coming tidal bore

And you can see silver mountains twenty times more.

II

The wind blows rain into the Pavilion slant-wise,

Fine verse should be composed in praise of the grand view.

After the rain the sea turns green, no tide will rise,

The lightening flashes like a snake of golden hue.

三

青山断处塔层层,
隔岸人家唤欲鹰④。
江上秋风晚来急,
为传钟鼓列西兴⑤。

④鹰:同"应",回应。
⑤西兴:即西陵,相传为范蠡屯兵处。

III

Where blue hills sever, there stands a pagoda tall,

People on either shore answer each other's call.

The strong wind in an autumn evening will bring

The sound of ringing bells and beating drums to Xixing.

八月十五日看潮五绝

一

定知玉兔[①]十分圆,
已作霜风九月寒。
寄语重门[②]休上钥[③],
夜潮留向月中看。

二

万人鼓噪[④]慑[⑤]吴侬[⑥],
犹是浮江老阿童[⑦]。
欲识潮头高几许,
越山浑[⑧]在浪花中。

①玉兔:指月亮。
②重门:九重天门。
③钥:锁。
④鼓噪:击鼓喊叫。
⑤慑:震慑。
⑥吴侬:吴人。
⑦阿童:晋王濬,小名阿童,平蜀以后,他造战船、练水军,顺流东下,消灭了东吴。
⑧浑:全。

　　钱塘江大潮自古以来被称为"天下奇观"。此组观潮绝句,第一首点明时间与打算,第二首和第五首描绘潮水汹涌而来的壮丽景象和磅礴气势,第三首抒发感慨,第四首则发议论,通篇淋漓恣肆,意气盎然。最能体现其雄放之风的为第五首,不着一字实景,巧用"庄子秋水""夫差水犀手""钱镠射潮"的典故,于雄奇瑰丽的想象中描出钱塘江大潮惊心动魄的声色气势,令人观之动容,跨越千年时空仍能在头脑中栩栩如生呈现大潮之威。

Watching the Tidal Bore on Mid-autumn Festival

I

The moon with jade-rabbit must be full to behold,
As in ninth month, the wind is blowing frosty cold.
Tell the Moon Goddess not to lock her door tonight,
'Tis best to watch the tidal bore in the moonlight.

II

The Southerners are scared at ten thousand men's roar
As if downstream came conquerors' warships and glaives.
If you want to know how high is the tidal bore,
See the Southern hills mingle with white-crested waves.

三

江边身世两悠悠,

久与沧波共白头。

造物亦知人易老,

故教江水向西流。

四

吴儿生长狎⑨涛渊,

冒利轻生不自怜。

东海若知明主意,

应教斥卤⑩变桑田。

五

江神河伯两醯鸡⑪,

海若⑫东来气吐霓。

安得夫差⑬水犀手,

三千强弩射潮低!⑭

⑨狎(xiá):玩弄。
⑩斥卤:海边的盐碱地。
⑪醯(xī)鸡:小虫名。
⑫海若:海神。
⑬夫差:春秋时期吴王,此处借指五代时期的吴越王。
⑭"三千"句:苏轼自注:吴越王尝以弓弩射潮头,与海神战,自尔水不进城。

III

As water's flowing east, life is passing away,

Long since man has white hair and waves have their white crest.

The Creator fears lest our hair should too soon turn gray,

He orders the river to flow back to the west.

IV

The Southerners from birth are fond of playing with waves,

They make light of their lives for profits and for gains.

If the East Sea knew what our sage sovereign craves,

The salt water would change into ricefields and plains.

V

The two Gods of the River vie to raise the tide,

From the westward-rolling billows rainbows will spout.

Where could we find three thousand Wu archers to chide

The billows with arrows so that the tide flow out?

催试官考较^①戏作

八月十五夜,
月色随处好。
不择茅檐与市楼,
况我官居似蓬岛^②。
凤咮堂^③前野橘香,
剑潭桥畔秋荷老。
八月十八潮,
壮观天下无。
鲲鹏水击三千里,
组练^④长驱十万夫。
红旗青盖互明灭,
黑沙白浪相吞屠。

①考较：指考后阅卷。
②蓬岛：蓬莱仙岛。
③凤咮（zhòu）堂：在杭州凤凰山下。
④组练：指军队。

　　此诗是一首杂言古诗,作者监考贡举时作。按照宋制,贡举的考试放榜在中秋节这一日,这一年却迟了两天,难怪诗人要催试官赶快阅卷发榜。可诗人并不明着催,而是从中秋夜月起笔,再以钱塘江大潮之壮观相诱,提醒试官们误了

Written to Examiners in Joke

On the mid-autumn night

Everywhere the moon is bright,

Over the thatched roof, over the city hall,

Over my mansion which looks like a fairy-land,

O'er the Sword Pool where lotus blooms grow old in the fall,

O'er the Phoenix Beak where wild oranges fragrant stand.

On the eighteenth of the eighth moon,

Incomparable high tide at noon:

Like water spouted three thousand miles high by whales

Or the march of ten myriads of armored men.

Red flags and blue canopies furl and unfurl like sails;

Black sand and white waves swallow each other now and then.

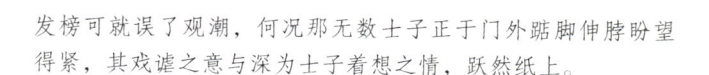

发榜可就误了观潮,何况那无数士子正于门外踮脚伸脖盼望得紧,其戏谑之意与深为士子着想之情,跃然纸上。

人生会合古难必,
此景此行那两得!
愿君闻此添蜡烛,
门外白袍⑤如立鹄⑥。

⑤白袍:指未仕的士子,宋代没有官职的人依制度穿白袍。
⑥立鹄(hú):像天鹅一样引颈跷脚站立,盼望等待的样子。

'Tis hard for men to get together as of old,

Candidates would regret not to see such a scene.

I hope you will burn more candles as you are told,

For outdoors candidates craning their necks can be seen.

法惠寺[1]横翠阁

朝见吴山[2]横,
暮见吴山纵。
吴山故多态,
转折为君容。
幽人[3]起朱阁,
空洞更无物。
惟有千步冈[4],
东西作帘额。
春来故国归无期,
人言秋悲春更悲。
已泛平湖[5]思濯锦[6],
更看横翠忆峨眉。

[1]法惠寺:在杭州清波门外,五代时吴越王钱镠所建。
[2]吴山:位于今杭州市西南。
[3]幽人:隐士。
[4]千步冈:指吴山。
[5]平湖:指西湖。
[6]濯(zhuó)锦:即成都的锦江,岷江分支之一。

此诗前八句五言写景,后十句七言抒情,借鉴民间歌谣重叠而略有变化的句式,韵脚平仄交错,读来谐和悦耳却渐生怆然之情。眼见吴山纵横多态,转思故乡濯锦峨眉;乡思已起却归家无期,继而慨叹人生短暂兴废无常……通篇由景

The Recumbent Green Pavilion of Fahui Temple

At dawn I see the hills recumbent lie;

At dusk I see them towering high.

It is true these green hills are full of grace,

Trying to please you by changing their face.

A recluse has built a pavilion here,

With nothing round but solitude far and near

And this ridge with its thousand-pace-high crest

Extending curtain-like from east to west.

Spring comes but brings for me not a home-coming dream;

If autumn is sad, then spring is much sadder still.

On the lake I recall the Brocade-washing Stream;

And of Mount Brows reminds me the recumbent hill.

及情、由情归景,波澜起伏、前呼后应,思绪如风筝,起之由风,落之由风,唯余今古慨叹:念天地之悠悠,独怆然而涕下。

雕栏能得几时好,
不独凭栏人易老。
百年兴废更堪哀,
悬知⁷草莽化池台。
游人寻我旧游处,
但觅吴山横处来。

⑦悬知:事先知道。

How long can the carved railings be good to behold?

The man who leans on them will easily grow old.

More lamentable is dynastic rise and fall!

We can foretell briers will grow in this painted hall.

If a rambler looks for the place where have rambled I,

He'll but find the recumbent hills before his eye.

冬至日独游吉祥寺[1]

井底微阳回未回，
萧萧寒雨湿枯荄[2]。
何人更似苏夫子，
不是花时肯独来。

[1]吉祥寺：即杭州广福寺。
[2]荄（gāi）：草根。

    寒冷的冬至，万物凋零，苏轼独游曾经牡丹花开、繁花似锦的吉祥寺，无花无人备感冷清。然而诗人并未停思于这萧瑟清冷，正所谓"冬天来了，春天还会远吗？"，枯萎的草根意味着阳气回升后的重生。繁花固然热闹，冷清却令人清醒，追名逐利还是洗尽铅华？天下熙熙攘攘，有多少人能像苏夫子：不是花时肯独来？好问题。

Visiting Alone the Temple of Auspicious Fortune on Winter Solstice

In the depth of the well warmth has not yet come back,

Showers of cold rain have wetted withered grass root.

No one would come to visit the Temple for there lack

Flowers in full bloom, but alone I come on foot.

书双竹^①湛师房（二首选一）

暮鼓朝钟自击撞，
闭门孤枕对残釭^②。
白灰旋拨通红火，
卧听萧萧雪打窗。

①双竹：即杭州广严寺。
②釭（gāng）：油灯。

晨钟暮鼓身外事，闭门孤枕自起息。诗人游宿山寺，拨灰听雨，独对内心洗凡尘，多少事欲说还休！孤枕残灯却有通红火暖，风雨萧萧只须隔窗卧听，宁静清淡中见超脱旷达，其味隽永。

Written for the Meditation Room of the Abbot of the Double Bamboo Monastery

You beat your evening drum and ring your morning bell,

Doors closed, a pillow facing a lamp, you rest well.

After poking among gray ashes embers red,

You hear snow-flakes fall shower by shower while abed.

吴中①田妇叹

今年粳②稻熟苦迟,
庶③见霜风来几时。
霜风来时雨如泻,
杷④头出菌⑤镰生衣。
眼枯泪尽雨不尽,
忍见黄穗卧青泥!
茅苫⑥一月陇上宿,
天晴获稻随车归。
汗流肩赪⑦载入市,
价贱乞与如糠粞⑧。
卖牛纳税拆屋炊,
虑浅不及明年饥。

①吴中:江浙一带。
②粳(jīng):俗称"大米"。
③庶:差不多。
④杷(pá):同"耙",农作时翻土的工具。
⑤出菌:发霉。
⑥茅苫(shān):茅棚,苫,草帘子。
⑦赪(chēng):红色。
⑧粞(xī):碎米。

这是一首仿新乐府的诗,写于江南秋雨成灾的背景之下,苏轼时任杭州通判。诗人借田妇之口,一叹稻熟迟,二叹雨成灾,三叹谷价贱——处处伤农,无有活路!民不堪其苦,吏却罔顾死活,激愤里流露出诗人对王安石新法的不满,更

Lament of a Peasant Woman Living in the South of the River

To our sorrow the rice ripens so late this year,
And soon we will see the frosty autumn wind blow.
Before the frosty wind the rain pours far and near,
The sickles rust and on the rake's teeth mold will grow.
Can we bear to see golden stalks flat in mud deep?
Though we weep our eyes dry, yet the rain never stops.
In a straw shelter by the fields one month we sleep,
Once it clears, our cart comes back loaded with our crops.
Sweaty, we carry them on our shoulders chafed red
To the market where at the price of chaff they're sold.
To pay the tax we sell the ox and pull down the shed
For fuel and next year's hunger can be foretold.

饱含着东坡对民生疾苦的深切忧虑与同情。全篇情感丰沛，农民劳动生活的场景如历历在目，其悲苦无着亦令人沉痛彻骨。

官今要钱不要米,
西北万里招羌儿。
龚黄⑨满朝人更苦,
不如却作河伯妇⑩!

⑨龚黄:龚遂、黄霸,皆为汉代清官。此处指推行新法的官员,是反语。
⑩河伯妇:此处用"河伯娶妻"的典故,犹言不如投河,一死了之。

In cash instead of in kind the tax should be paid
So that tribesmen be bought o'er on northwest frontier.
The peasants suffer more for wise reforms just made,
They would rather be drowned than live in such a year.

於潜①女

青裙缟袂②於潜女,
两足如霜不穿屦③,
觰沙④鬓发丝穿杼⑤,
蓬沓障前走风雨。
老濞⑥官妆传父祖,
至今遗民悲故主。
苕溪⑦杨柳初飞絮,
照溪画眉渡溪去。
逢郎樵归相媚妩,
不信姬姜有齐鲁。

①於潜:浙江古县名。
②缟袂(gǎo mèi):白衣。
③屦(jù):鞋。
④觰(zhā)沙:张开。
⑤杼(zhù):织布机的梭子。
⑥老濞(bì):汉吴王刘濞,此借指五代十国的吴越王。
⑦苕溪:位于浙江省北部,是浙江省八大水系之一。

诗人以乐府民歌般古朴自然的风格,为我们白描出一幅以於潜女为主题的乡村风景画。梳越王宫妆发式,着青裙白衫,露白皙赤足行走风雨,寥寥几笔勾勒出於潜女天生丽质与古风浓厚的妆式所融合的美;临溪画眉、逢郎媚妩,则再

A Country-woman of Yuqian

A country-woman in farm dress and skirt blue
Reveals her frost-white bare feet for she wears no shoe.
A silver hairpin passing through her tousled hair,
Like shuttle in a loom she wades in wind and rain.
Hers is the dress that ancient palace maids did wear:
People cannot forget their former master's reign.
Willow catkins begin to fly beside the brook
Which sees her pass across with her pencilled eyebrows.
The woodman comes back, they exchange an amorous look
And won't believe on earth there is a happier spouse.

添其大胆淳真与热烈奔放;"不信姬姜有齐鲁",这样质朴无邪又健康活力的乡村女子不相信齐鲁姬姜的富贵华美,可又何须相信!她们自无忧无虑,她们自得其乐,她们自美其美!

行香子·过七里濑[1]

一叶舟轻,
双桨鸿惊。
水天清、影湛[2]波平。
鱼翻藻鉴[3],
鹭点烟汀。
过沙溪急,
霜溪冷,
月溪明。

[1]七里濑(lài):又名七里滩,在今浙江省桐庐县。濑,沙石上流过的急水。
[2]湛:清澈。
[3]藻鉴:背面刻有藻纹的铜镜,这里指像镜子一样的水面。

这首词将物是人非、人生如梦的深沉感喟,融化在七里濑的水光山色之中,表现出作者否定功名利禄和皈心大自然的思想感情。作者用白描兼比喻的手法写景,上片写水,下片写山,笔墨简洁,动静交错,意象幽美空灵,令人神往。全篇用线状铺叙法,江上各种景物顺次呈现,显出舟行的动态流程,创造出空明清幽意境。上下片结尾总写溪山之不同景色,排比精妙,意象优美,音节响亮,令人心旷神怡。

Song of Pilgrimage
Passing the Seven-league Shallows

A leaf-like boat goes light,

At dripping oars wild geese take fright.

Under a sky serene

Clear shadows float on calm waves green.

Among the mirrored water grass fish play

And egrets dot the riverbank mist-gray.

Thus I go past

The sandy brook flowing fast,

The frosted brook cold,

The moonlit brook bright to behold.

重重似画,
曲曲如屏。
算当年、虚老严陵④。
君臣⑤一梦,
今古空名。
但远山长,
云山乱,
晓山青。

④严陵:即严光,字子陵,东汉人,年轻时曾与光武帝刘秀一同游学。刘秀称帝后,他改名隐居。
⑤君臣:指刘秀和严光。

Hill upon hill is a picturesque scene;

Bend after bend looks like a screen.

I recall those far-away years:

The hermit wasted his life till he grew old;

The emperor shared the same dream with his peers.

Then as now, their fame was left out in the cold.

Only the distant hills outspread

Till they're unseen,

The cloud-crowned hills look dishevelled

And dawn-lit hills so green.

行香子·丹阳①寄述古②

携手江村,
梅雪飘裙。
情何限?
处处销魂!
故人③不见,
旧曲重闻。
向望湖楼,
孤山寺,
涌金门。

① 丹阳:今江苏省丹阳市。
② 述古:杭州知州陈襄,字述古。
③ 故人:指陈述古。

　　友人携歌妓探梅寻春,在望湖楼、孤山寺、涌金门等风景胜地,重闻旧曲,一定会忆念曾经同游的我。观看寺壁题诗时,歌妓用红袖拂去我诗壁上的尘埃,友人在旁一边读诗一边思念我。思念我的恐怕还有杭州的湖中月、江边柳、陇头云。整首词构思独特,通过对方如何思念自己,从而表达自己忆念友人的感情。

Song of Pilgrimage
Reminiscence

We visited riverside village hand in hand,

Letting snowlike mume flowers on silk dress fall.

How can I stand

The soul-consuming fairy land!

Now severed from you for years long,

Hearing the same old song,

Can I forget the lakeside hall,

The temple on the Lonely Hill

And Golden Gate waves overfill?

寻常行处,
题诗千首,
绣罗衫、
与拂红尘。
别来相忆,
知是何人?
有湖④中月,
江边柳,
陇⑤头云。

④湖:指杭州西湖。
⑤陇:田埂。

Wherever we went on whatever day,

We have written a thousand lines.

The silken sleeves would sweep the dust away.

Since we parted, who

Would often think of you?

The moon which on the lake shines,

The lakeside willow trees,

The cloud and breeze.

行香子·述怀

清夜无尘,
月色如银。
酒斟时、须满十分①。
浮名浮利,
虚苦劳神。
叹隙中驹,
石中火,
梦中身。

①十分:指斟酒满盏。

  这首词上片抒发对名利虚浮、人生短暂的感慨;下片表达要摆脱世俗困扰,归隐田园,回归纯真本性的心愿。词从月夜起笔,营造了一个清净、无尘杂、无欲求的氛围。全篇即在这种氛围中展开。特别是上下片各用三个排比的意象,分别形容人生的短促和隐居生活的清闲,生动贴切,代入感极强。

Song of Pilgrimage Reflections

Stainless in the clear night;

The moon is silver bright.

Fill my wine cup

Till it brims up!

Why toil with pain

For wealth and fame in vain?

Time flies as a steed white

Passes a gap in flight.

Like a spark in the dark

Or a dream of moonbeam.

虽抱文章,
开口谁亲?
且陶陶②、乐尽天真。
几时归去?
作个闲人。
对一张琴,
一壶酒,
一溪云。

②陶陶:无忧无虑、单纯快乐的样子。

Though I can write,

Who thinks I'm right?

Why not enjoy

Like a mere boy?

So I would be

A man carefree.

I would be mute before my lute;

Fine before wine;

And proud as cloud.

醉落魄·离京口①作

轻云微月，
二更②酒醒船初发。
孤城回望苍烟合。
记得歌时，
不记归时节。

巾偏扇坠藤床滑，
觉来幽梦无人说。
此生飘零何时歇？
家在西南，
常作东南别。

①京口：今江苏省镇江市。
②二更：晚上九时至十一时。

    这首词创作于公元1074年，彼时苏轼在润州完成赈灾事宜后，从京口返回杭州，临行之际挥笔而就。词人从沉醉中苏醒，回忆起那欢歌笑语的晚宴场景，以及巾偏扇坠、藤床滑溜的醉态模样。在似梦非梦之间，词人感慨万千，故乡远在西南之地的眉山，如今却要向东南方向道别。羁旅漂泊，心中兀自神伤；仕宦奔波，顿生倦怠之感，思归之情愈发急切。

Drunk with Soul Lost
Leaving the Riverside Town

The crescent moon veiled by cloud light,
I wake from wine when my boat sets sail at midnight.
Turning my head toward the mist-veiled lonely town,
I only remember the farewell song,
But not when from the wineshop I got down.

Hood wry, fan dropped, I slipped from wicker bed.
Whom can I tell the dreary dream I dread?
When from this floating life may I take rest?
My hometown in southwest,
Why do I oft in southeast bid adieu as guest?

醉落魄·苏州阊门①留别

苍颜华发,
故山归计何时决?
旧交新贵音书绝。
惟有佳人②,
犹作殷勤别。

离亭③欲去歌声咽,
潇潇细雨凉吹颊。
泪珠不用罗巾浥④。
弹在罗衫,
图得见时说。

①阊(chāng)门:苏州古城之西门。
②佳人:指歌女。
③离亭:驿路边的亭子。
④浥(yì):湿润。

阊门,苏州西门,地近运河,别筵在此举行。开篇"苍颜华发",道出词人因政治失意而未老先衰之感。不得志,思乡之情更迫切。可"我亦恋薄禄,因循失归休"。人情冷暖,唯有同有不幸命运的歌妓与词人惜别。细雨、热泪,"图得见时说",以期待重聚的劝慰作结,赋予歌妓词新的灵魂和生命。

Drunk with Soul Lost
Farewell at the Gate of Suzhou

A pale face with hair grey,

When can I go home without care?

No word's received from my friends old or new,

Only the songstress fair

Comes to sing for me a song of adieu.

On leaving the pavilion, with sobs she sings;

The chilly breeze a drizzling rain to my cheeks brings.

Don't use your handkerchief to wipe your tears away!

Let them fall on your silken sleeves!

When we meet again, I know how it grieves.

南乡子·送述古

回首乱山横,
不见居人只见城。
谁似临平山①上塔,
亭亭,
迎客西来送客行。

归路晚风清,
一枕初寒梦不成。
今夜残灯斜照处,
荧荧②,
秋雨晴时泪不晴。

①临平山:位于杭州东北,山上有临平塔,时为送别的标志。
②荧荧:既指灯光,也指泪光。

　　这首词上片写行人途中回望,只见乱山、城池,不见城中故人。既表现出送行之远和行人对旧地的依恋,又暗用典故赞颂陈述古。接着,用拟人化无情之山塔为有情之物,从而衬托自己惜别情意之深。下片直叙归来之凄清景色、归后不寐、入夜之悲,其思念之情,可谓情味深长。

Song of Southern Country
Farewell to a Friend

Turning my head, I find rugged mountains bar the sky,

I can no longer see you in the town.

Who can be like the hilltop tower looking down,

So high?

It welcomed you from the west and bids you goodbye.

I come back at dusk in a gentle breeze.

On chilly pillow how can I dream with ease?

Where will the flickering lamp shed its lonely light tonight?

When autumn rain no longer falls drop by drop,

Oh, will tears stop?

南乡子·梅花词和杨元素[1]

寒雀满疏篱,
争抱寒柯[2]看玉蕤[3]。
忽见客来花下坐,
惊飞。
蹋散芳英落酒卮[4]。

痛饮又能诗,
坐客无毡醉不知。
花尽酒阑春到也,
离离[5]。
一点微霜已著枝。

[1]杨元素:即杨绘,字元素。苏轼作杭州通判时,杨元素是知州。
[2]柯:树枝。
[3]蕤(ruí):花朵繁盛的样子。
[4]酒卮(zhī):酒杯。
[5]离离:浓密的样子。

  寒雀踏枝赏梅,文人树下观花,雀惊枝颤,梅瓣落杯,真一幅妙趣、雅趣交叠的冬雪赏梅图。鸟之活泼、梅之清冷、人之欢笑,这盎然生机落在诗人眼中、笔下、心怀,愉悦之意渐次浓烈,继而痛饮、醉卧,全然不知。
  思想深刻者,热爱盎然的生机!

Song of Southern Country
Mume Blossoms for Yang Yuansu

On the fence perch birds feeling cold,

To view the blooms of jade they dispute for branch old.

Seeing a guest sit under flowers, they fly up

And scatter petals over his wine cup.

Writing verses and drinking wine,

The guest knows not he's not sitting on felt fine.

Wine cup dried up, spring comes with fallen flower.

Leave here! The branch has felt a little sour.

江城子·湖上与张先①同赋②

凤凰山③下雨初晴。
水风清。
晚霞明。
一朵芙蕖④、开过尚盈盈⑤。
何处飞来双白鹭?
如有意,
慕娉婷⑥。

忽闻江上弄哀筝。
苦含情。
遣谁听?
烟敛云收、依约是湘灵⑦。

①张先:字子野,乌程(今浙江湖州)人。北宋著名词人。
②同赋:用同一词牌,取同一题材填词。
③凤凰山:在杭州西湖之南。
④芙蕖(qú):即已经开放的荷花。
⑤盈盈:美丽轻盈的样子。
⑥娉婷:形容女子的美好姿态。
⑦湘灵:传说中的湘水之神。

时为杭州通判的苏轼与词人张先同游西湖,闻有人弹筝,即兴而作。全词紧扣闻弹筝这一词题,从多方面描写弹筝人的美好与悦耳的音乐。雨后初晴、晚霞明丽的湖光山色中,风韵娴雅、绰有态度的弹筝人,如盈盈荷花,筝音一起,竟

Riverside Town
On the Lake

It turns fine after rain below the Phoenix Hill,

Waves and wind light,

Rainbow clouds bright.

A lotus flower past full bloom beams with smile still.

Where comes in flight

A pair of egrets white

As if inclined to care

For maidens fair.

Suddenly on the stream music comes to the ear.

Who would not hear

Such feeling drear?

Away clouds and mist clear;

The Spirit of River Xiang seems to appear.

引来双鹭倾听。其实，双鹭喻指二客。下阕重点写音乐，一个哀筝奠定基调。乐曲哀伤，谁能忍听，烟霭敛容，云彩收色，如湘水女神倾诉哀伤。结句写弹筝人飘然远逝，只余青翠山峰静静聆听荡漾于山间水际的哀怨余音。

欲待曲终寻问取,
人不见,
数峰青。

When music ends, I would inquire for the lutist dear.

She seems to disappear,

Only leaving peaks clear.

昭君怨·送别

谁作桓伊①三弄,
惊破绿窗②幽梦?
新月与愁烟,
满江天。

欲去又还不去,
明日落花飞絮。
飞絮送行舟,
水东流。

① 桓伊:东晋时音乐家,善吹笛。
② 绿窗:罩有碧纱的窗子,多指女子居室。

    此词上片写送别情景,以景色为笛声的背景,情景交融地渲染出送别时的感伤氛围;下片运用叠句造境传情,想象来日分别的情景,大大扩展了离情别绪的空间。通观全词,没有写一句惜别的话,没有强烈激切的抒情,只将情感融入景物,虚实结合,渲染出一种强烈的情感氛围。

Lament of a Fair Lady

Who's playing on the flute a gloomy tune:
Breaking the green window's dreary dream?
The dreary mist veils the new moon.
Outspread in the sky over the stream.

You linger still though you must go.
Afraid flowers and willow down will fall tomorrow.
How could the stream not eastward flow?
Let willow down follow your boat laden with sorrow!

瑞鹧鸪·观潮

碧山影里小红旗,
侬是江南踏浪儿①。
拍手欲嘲山简②醉,
齐声争唱浪婆③词。

西兴渡口帆初落,
渔浦山头日未欹④。
侬欲送潮歌底⑤曲,
樽前还唱使君⑥诗。

①踏浪儿:参加水戏的人。
②山简:字季伦,晋人,好酒。
③浪婆:波浪之神。
④欹(qī):倾斜。
⑤底:什么。
⑥使君:指杭州知州陈襄。

  浙江钱塘潮本是大自然的奇观,自唐以来,天下闻名。身为杭州通判的苏轼自然要前去观赏,这首词便是其观潮后所作。上片,苏轼仅描写了钱塘潮中弄潮儿在万顷波中自由、活泼的形象,展现出乐观、开朗的精神状态。下片写退潮,弄潮儿唱起"使君诗"作为送潮曲。渡口落帆、山头红日等静态的景物,既显示出时间的推移,又暗写钱江已退潮。词人用笔精练、表达含蓄。

Auspicious Partridge
Watching the Tidal Bore

In the shade of blue hills small red flags undulate,
You are sons of the Southerners treading waves green.
Clapping your hands, you laugh at the drunk magistrate;
In unison, you vie to sing "Goddess Marine".

Sails have just lowered down in the Ferry Xixing;
Atop Yupu hills the sun begins to decline.
If you want to see the tide fall, what will you sing?
It's your magistrate's song before a cup of wine.

虞美人·有美堂赠述古

湖山信是东南美，
一望弥千里。
使君能得几回来？
便使樽前醉倒、更徘徊。

沙河塘①里灯初上，
水调谁家唱？
夜阑风静欲归时，
惟有一江明月、碧琉璃②。

①沙河塘：位于杭州东南。
②碧琉璃：绿色的玻璃。形容江水之澄澈。

    一望千里的湖光山色，尽在有美堂周遭。览景兴怀，即席抒情。此值杭州知州陈述古将罢任远去，惜别志同道合的上司，于有美堂设宴。华灯初上，觥筹交错中，唯求酩酊大醉少别愁。结尾一句，不仅写出月明水净的夜景，同时也展示了词人一无杂虑的澄澈心境。

The Beautiful Lady Yu
Written for Chen Xiang at the Scenic Hall

How fair the lakes and hills of the Southeast land are,
With plains extending wide and far!
How oft, wine-cup in hand, have you been here
That you can make us linger though drunk we appear?

By Sandy River Pond the new-lit lamps are bright.
Who is singing "the water melody" at night?
When I come back, the wind goes down, the bright moon paves
With emerald glass the river waves.

少年游·润州[1]作,代人寄远

去年相送,
余杭门[2]外,
飞雪似杨花。
今年春尽,
杨花似雪,
犹不见还家。

对酒卷帘邀明月,
风露透窗纱。
恰似姮娥[3]怜双燕,
分明照、画梁斜。

①润州:今江苏省镇江市。
②余杭门:北宋时杭州北门之一。
③姮娥:即嫦娥,亦指月亮。

  1074年四月初,词人在润州赈灾,久别未归,故假托妻子王闰之思念行役在外的自己而作此词。借思妇诉说分别的时间、地点,传达彼此的惦念。从飞雪似杨花到杨花似雪的时间变换中,词人将别离之久、牵挂之甚,淋漓表达。下片将姮娥与妻子类比,虚实结合道出思念的孤苦凄冷。同时,其怜悯的光辉洒向画梁上的燕巢,双燕更惹人产生思念之情。

Wandering Youth
Written for a Friend

Last year we bade adieu

Outside the town;

Snow flew like willow down.

This year spring dies,

Like snow willow down flies,

But I can't come back to see you.

The screen uprolled, to wine I invite the moon bright;

Through the window the breeze brings in dew.

The Moon Goddess seems to care

For the swallows in pair.

She sheds her light

Into their dream on painted beam.

腊日游孤山访惠勤惠思二僧

天欲雪,
云满湖,
楼台明灭①山有无。
水清出石鱼可数,
林深无人鸟相呼②。
腊日不归对妻孥③,
名④寻道人⑤实自娱。
道人之居在何许?
宝云山⑥前路盘纡⑦。
孤山孤绝谁肯庐?
道人有道山不孤。

①明灭:若隐若现。
②鸟相呼:群鸟相和而鸣。
③妻孥(nú):妻子和子女的统称。
④名:名义上。
⑤道人:此处指和尚。
⑥宝云山:山名,位于西湖北面。
⑦纡(yū):弯曲。

全诗围绕"游"和"访"二字铺开,将游孤山与访二僧结合,写出了此次游访的清欢、兴致盎然。诗人将更多的笔墨放在了写景上,景是实景,而访僧人的内容更多的是虚写,给人留下无限想象的空间。云雪楼台、游鱼水石、深林啼鸟、盘纡山路、纸窗竹屋、连绵林木、鹘盘浮图,有景有物,动

Visiting in Winter the Two Learned Monks in the Lonely Hill

It seems that snow will fall

On a cloud-covered lake,

Hills loom and fade, towers appear and disappear.

Fish can be count'd among the rocks in water clear;

Birds call back and forth in the deep woods men forsake.

I cannot go home on this lonely winter day,

So I visit the monks to while my time away.

Who can show me the way which leads to their door-sill?

Follow the winding path to the foot of the hill.

The Lonely Hill is so lonesome. Who will dwell there?

Strong in faith, there's no loneliness but they can bear.

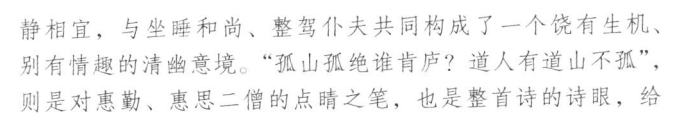

静相宜,与坐睡和尚、整驾仆夫共同构成了一个饶有生机、别有情趣的清幽意境。"孤山孤绝谁肯庐?道人有道山不孤",则是对惠勤、惠思二僧的点睛之笔,也是整首诗的诗眼,给人留下了极其深刻的难以忘却的印象。

纸窗竹屋深自暖,
拥褐坐睡依团蒲。
天寒路远愁仆夫,
整驾催归及未晡⁸。
出山回望云木合,
但见野鹘盘浮图⁹。
兹游淡薄欢有馀,
到家恍⁽¹⁰⁾如梦蘧蘧⁽¹¹⁾。
作诗火急追亡逋⁽¹²⁾,
清景一失后难摹。

⑧晡(bū):申时,黄昏之前。
⑨浮图:佛塔。
⑩恍:恍惚。
⑪蘧(qú)蘧:惊动的样子。
⑫亡逋(bū):逃亡者。

Paper windows keep them warm in bamboo cottage deep;

Sitting in their coarse robes, on round rush mats they sleep.

My lackeys grumble at cold weather and long road,

They hurry me to go before dusk to my abode.

Leaving the hill, I look back and see woods and cloud

Mingled and wild birds circling the pagoda proud.

This trip has not tired me but left an aftertaste,

Come back, I seem to see in dreams the scene retraced.

I hasten to write down in verse what I saw then,

For the scene lost to sight can't be revived again.

江城子·孤山竹阁送述古

翠蛾羞黛怯人看，
掩霜纨①，
泪偷弹。
且尽一尊，
收泪唱《阳关》②。
漫道帝城天样远，
天易见，
见君难。

① 霜纨（wán）：指白纨扇。纨，细绢。
②《阳关》：即《阳关曲》，著名的送别歌曲。

苏轼任杭州通判的第三个年头，知州陈述古由杭州调至陈州，此词便系孤山竹阁离别筵席上所作。上片写送别的情景，歌妓悲伤落泪的情态，以及留恋之情。下片抒发相思之情，画堂新建，将无人共赏，并想象来年春日再棹舟西湖也难觅旧迹欢踪，情意无穷。此词构思独特，从歌妓角度着笔，将歌妓的情态和心理描摹得细致入微，栩栩如生，寄寓了词人对友人的深情厚谊、离别的惆怅和依依不舍之情。

Riverside Town
Farewell to Governor Chen at Bamboo Pavilion on Lonely Hill

Her eyebrows penciled dark, she feels shy to be seen.

Hidden behind a silken fan so green,

Stealthily she sheds tear on tear.

Let me drink farewell to you and hear

Her sing, with tears wiped away, her song of adieu.

Do not say the imperial town is as far as the sky.

It is easier to see the sun high

Than to meet you.

画堂新构近孤山,
曲栏干,
为谁安?
飞絮落花,
春色属③明年。
欲棹④小舟寻旧事,
无处问,
水连天。

③属:同"嘱",嘱托。
④棹(zhào):船桨。用作动词,意为划船。

The newly built painted hall to Lonely Hill is near.

For whom is made

The winding balustrade?

Falling flowers and willow down fly;

Spring belongs to next year.

I try to row a boat to find the things gone by.

O whom can I ask? In my eye

I only see water one with the sky.

密州

老夫聊发少年狂

沁园春·赴密州，早行，马上寄子由

孤馆灯青，
野店鸡号，
旅枕梦残。
渐月华收练①，
晨霜耿耿②；
云山摛锦③，
朝露漙漙④。
世路无穷，
劳生有限，
似此区区长鲜欢。
微吟⑤罢，
凭征鞍⑥无语，
往事千端⑦。

①练：白绢，形容月光。
②耿耿：明亮的样子。
③摛（chī）锦：像锦缎一样展开。
④漙（tuán）漙：露水很多的样子。
⑤微吟：小声吟哦。
⑥征鞍：指旅者所乘的马。
⑦千端：千头万绪。

这首词抒写政治情怀，抒发了辅君济世的远大抱负及其不得实现的牢骚。其中有怅惘，有坚定，有酸痛，有豁达。上片描绘了一幅清丽、凄冷、寂寞的秋日早行图，并引出世路艰辛的感叹。下片直抒胸臆，追述昔年抱负，折转到当前困顿失意，最后以旷达自适的处世态度自我解脱并劝慰子由。

Spring in a Pleasure Garden
Written to Ziyou on My Way to Mizhou

The lamp burns with green flames in an inn's lonely hall,

The wayfarer's dream is broken by the cock's call.

Slowly the blooming moon rolls up her silk dress white,

The frost begins to shimmer in the soft daylight;

The cloud-crowned hills outspread their brocade

And morning dews glitter like pearls displayed.

As the way of the world is long,

But our toilsome life short,

So, for a man like me, joyless is oft my sort.

After humming this song,

Silent, on my saddle I lean,

Brooding over the past scene after scene.

当时共客长安⁸,
似二陆⁹初来俱少年。
有笔头千字,
胸中万卷;
致君尧舜⁽¹⁰⁾,
此事何难!
用舍由时,
行藏⁽¹¹⁾在我,
袖手何妨闲处看。
身长健,
但优游卒岁,
且斗樽前。

⑧共客长安:苏轼、苏辙二人嘉祐年间客居汴京应试。长安,代指汴京。
⑨二陆:指西晋文学家陆机、陆云兄弟。
⑩致君尧舜:辅佐国君,使其成为圣明之主。
⑪行藏(cáng):做官和退隐。

Together then to the capital we came,

Like the two Brothers Lu of literary fame.

A fluent pen combined

With a widely-read mind,

Why could we not have helped the Crown

To attain great renown?

As times require,

I advance or retire,

With folded arms I may stand by.

If we keep fit,

We may enjoy life before we lose it.

So drink the wine-cup dry!

江城子·密州出猎

老夫聊①发少年狂②,
左牵黄③,
右擎苍④。
锦帽貂裘,
千骑卷平冈。
为报倾城随太守,
亲射虎,
看孙郎⑤。

①聊:姑且。
②狂:豪情。
③黄:黄狗。
④苍:苍鹰。
⑤孙郎:孙权,作者自喻。

这首词借写打猎习武,抒发渴望为国杀敌立功的壮志豪情,在词的题材、内容、风格上都具有开创性。词中写他牵犬擎鹰狩猎的豪迈气概,写射猎武夫千骑如飞、倾城出动、围观如堵的场面,写孙权射虎、冯唐魏尚的典故,结尾处走马拉弓的特写镜头,多角度多侧面地勾勒、烘托,凸显出一

Riverside Town
Hunting at Mizhou

Rejuvenated, my fiery zeal I display:

Left hand leashing a yellow hound,

On the right wrist a falcon gray.

A thousand silk-capped and sable-coated horsemen sweep

Across the rising ground

And hillocks steep.

Townspeople come out of the city gate

To watch the tiger-hunting magistrate.

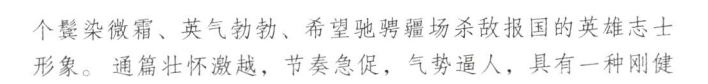

个鬓染微霜、英气勃勃、希望驰骋疆场杀敌报国的英雄志士形象。通篇壮怀激越，节奏急促，气势逼人，具有一种刚健豪迈的格调。

酒酣胸胆尚开张,
鬓微霜,
又何妨!
持节⑥云中,
何日遣冯唐?
会挽雕弓如满月,
西北望,
射天狼。

⑥节:兵符。

Heart gladdened with strong wine, who cares

For a few frosted hairs?

When will the imperial court send

Me as envoy with flags and banners? Then I'll bend

My bow like a full moon, and aiming northwest, I

Will shoot down the Wolf from the sky.

蝶恋花·密州上元

灯火钱塘三五夜[①],
明月如霜,
照见人如画。
帐底吹笙香吐麝[②],
更无一点尘随马。

寂寞山城[③]人老也,
击鼓吹箫,
却入农桑社。
火冷灯稀霜露下,
昏昏雪意云垂野。

① 三五夜:即每月十五日夜,此处指元宵节。
② 香吐麝:帐里吹出麝香的气味。
③ 山城:指密州。

东坡于熙宁七年(1074)九月离开杭州,十一月至密州任所。当时密州蝗旱灾相继,新法在执行中弊端丛生,使苏轼心情沉重,想起从前在杭州年节时候种种繁华热闹的情景,不禁加深了对杭州的怀恋之情。在上下片的对比描写中,以白描手法勾画出杭州和密州两地上元节时不同的景况:杭州是灯月交辉,花团锦簇,香飘乐裒,热闹喜悦;密州却是巷空人少,灯火冷落,云低欲雪,唯有一点疏落的箫鼓声点缀着山城的寂寞。全篇不用典,情意蕴含于景色画面之中。

Butterfly in Love with Flower
Lantern Festival at Mizhou

On Lantern Festival by riverside at night,

The moon frost-white

Shone on the beauties fair and bright.

Fragrance exhaled and music played under the tent,

The running horses raised no dust on the pavement.

Now I am old in lonely hillside town,

Drumbeats and flute songs up and down

Are drowned in prayers amid mulberries and lost.

The lantern fires put out, dew falls with frost.

Over the fields dark clouds hangs low:

It threatens snow.

水调歌头

丙辰中秋，欢饮达旦，大醉，作此篇，兼怀子由。

明月几时有？
把酒问青天。
不知天上宫阙①，
今夕是何年？
我欲乘风归去，
又恐琼楼玉宇，
高处不胜②寒。
起舞弄清影，
何似在人间？

①宫阙：月中宫殿。
②不胜：禁受不住。

这首词落笔高超，飘飘有凌云之气，极富浪漫色彩，被誉为中秋词中的咏月绝唱。除"转朱阁"三句实写外，都从自己问月、飞月、望月、怨月、慰月、舞月中虚笔写出，笔墨空灵洒脱，跌宕多姿。而中秋之月圆满、皎洁、清丽、高寒，月亮运行照临的动态，皆历历如在目前。上片写出世与

Prelude to Water Melody
Sent to Ziyou on Mid-autumn Festival

On the mid-autumn festival, I drank happily till dawn and wrote this in my cups while thinking of Ziyou.

When did the bright moon first appear?
Wine-cup in hand, I ask the blue sky.
I do not know what time of year
It would be tonight in the palace on high.
Riding the wind, there I would fly,
But I'm afraid the crystalline palace would be
Too high and too cold for me.
I rise and dance, with my shadow I play.
On high as on earth, would it be as gay?

入世、退隐与进取的矛盾心理,下片化景物为情思,最后化悲怨为旷达。词中表现出的善于自我解脱的达观襟怀,关于人生、自然、宇宙的睿智思考,以及结尾"但愿人长久,千里共婵娟"所蕴含的美好情感,皆能引发强烈的阅读共鸣。

转朱阁,
低绮户,
照无眠。
不应有恨,
何事③长向别时圆?
人有悲欢离合,
月有阴晴圆缺,
此事古难全。
但愿人长久,
千里共婵娟④。

③何事:为何,何故。
④婵娟:指月亮。

The moon goes round the mansions red

With gauze windows to shed

Her light upon the sleepless bed.

Against man she should not have any spite.

Why then when people part is she oft full and bright?

Men have sorrow and joy, they part and meet again;

The moon may be bright or dim, she may wax or wane.

There has been nothing perfect since olden days.

So let us wish that man live as long as he can!

Though miles apart, we'll share the beauty she displays.

江城子·乙卯正月二十日夜记梦

十年生死两茫茫,
不思量①,
自难忘。
千里孤坟,
无处话凄凉。
纵使相逢应不识:
尘满面,
鬓如霜。

①思量:想念。

用词写悼亡,是苏轼的首创。这首悼亡词,记录了梦中与亡妻王弗相会的情景,句句沉痛。词为记梦,全篇依梦前、梦中、梦后思路递进,写梦中的妻子在窗前梳妆打扮,二人相对无言唯有泪水涟涟等日常生活的情景细节,将现实的感受融入梦中,使真幻交织,催人泪下。而在怀旧悼亡中,作者又糅进了自己坎坷失意的身世之感,使词的情思意蕴更深厚,故而被古今词评家誉为千古第一悼亡词。

Riverside Town
Dreaming of My Deceased Wife on the Night of the 20th Day of the 1st Month

For ten long years the living of the dead knows nought.

Should the dead be forgot

And to mind never brought?

Her lonely grave is a thousand miles away.

To whom can I my grief convey?

Revived e'en if she be, could she still know me?

My face is worn with care

And frosted is my hair.

夜来幽梦忽还乡。

小轩②窗,

正梳妆。

相顾无言,

惟有泪千行。

料得年年肠断处:

明月夜,

短松冈。

②小轩:有窗的小屋。

Last night I dreamed of coming to my native place:

She's making up her face

At the window with grace.

We gazed at each other hushed,

But tears from our eyes gushed.

When I am woken, I fancy her heart-broken

On the mound clad with pines,

Where only the moon shines.

更漏子·送孙巨源[1]

水涵空[2],
山照市,
西汉二疏[3]乡里。
新白发,
旧黄金,
故人恩义深。

海东头,
山尽处,
自古客槎[4]来去。
槎有信,
赴秋期,
使君[5]行不归。

①孙巨源:孙洙,字巨源,苏轼朋友。
②涵空:指水映天空。
③西汉二疏:即疏广、疏受,二人为叔侄,均是西汉时的官吏,在任期间,多次受到皇帝赏赐。
④槎(chá):木筏。
⑤使君:指孙巨源。

1074年十月,苏轼在楚州(今江苏淮安)别孙巨源,借西汉请归受欢送的二疏故事,颂孙巨源在海州一邦留下的深恩厚庆。又以乘槎故事叙说别情:如今你"有信"应召进京,却归期无定相会无期。用典在苏词中常见,委婉意丰,曲折表达词人既庆贺又担忧的不安情绪。

Song of Water Clock
Seeing Sun Juyuan off

The water joins the sky,

The town girt with hills high,

This is a land of talents as of yore.

Your hair has turned white,

Of gold you make light,

You value friendship more.

East of the sea,

Where end the hills you see,

Boats come and go since days of old.

They have a date;

For you I'll wait.

Will you come back with autumn cold?

永遇乐·寄孙巨源

长忆别时,
景疏楼①上,
明月如水。
美酒清歌,
留连不住,
月随人千里。
别来三度②,
孤光又满,
冷落共谁同醉?
卷珠帘、凄然顾影,
共伊到明无寐。

①景疏楼:位于海州(在今江苏省连云港市)东北。
②三度:指三度月圆。

苏轼此词通篇借设想之辞,写人写己,无不倾诉怀念之情。上片想象孙巨源初别海州,明月有情,千里相共,照影无眠。词人设想友人在月下的心理感受,着力刻画,表面映托巨源,实写自己的怀人之思。情致细腻,思念深沉。

Joy of Eternal Union
For Sun Juyuan

I long remember when we bade goodbye

On Northeast Tower high,

The silvery moonlight looked like water bright.

But songs and wine, however fine,

Could not keep you from going away.

Only the moon followed you for miles on your way.

Since we parted, I've seen the moon wax and wane.

But who would drink with lonely me again?

Uprolling the screen,

Only my shadow's seen,

I stay awake until daybreak.

今朝有客,
来从潍③上,
能道使君深意。
凭仗清淮,
分明到海,
中有相思泪。
而今何在?
西垣④清禁⑤,
夜永露华⑥侵被⑦。
此时看、回廊晓月,
也应暗记。

③潍(suī):水名,自河南经安徽,流至江苏。
④西垣:中书省。
⑤清禁:宫中。当时孙巨源在宫中办公,故云。
⑥露华:露水。
⑦侵被:沾湿了被子。

Today your friend comes from the river's end,

And brings to me your memory

You ask the river clear

To bring nostalgic tear

As far as the east sea.

I do not know now where are you.

In palace hall by western wall,

Is your coverlet in deep night wet with dew?

When you see in the corridor the moving moonrays,

Could you forget the bygone days?

徐州

问言豆叶几时黄

阳关曲·中秋作

暮云收尽溢①清寒,
银汉②无声转玉盘③。
此生此夜不长好,
明月明年何处看?

①溢:满出,指月色如水。
②银汉:银河。
③玉盘:月亮。

云收则月现,不实写月,却道"溢清寒"。清寒何来?月色也。银河星辰绕月而行,本应有声却无声,可见天宇辽阔无极。明明是赏月,却将这思绪扩散至无边天际,天辽地远人圆,相聚之喜无边。

下阕却一转笔墨,深透别离之伤。

诗成于熙宁十年(1077),兄弟相聚徐州,苏辙《水调歌头·徐州中秋》云:"离别一何久,七度过中秋。"七载别离短暂相聚,如此人月共圆的良辰却不长久,明年明月虽在,人却远隔天际,唯有清寒无极,相思无极。

诗题"中秋",本应是人月圆;然调寄《阳关》,却是诉离别。伤!伤!伤!

Song of the Sunny Pass
The Mid-autumn Moon

Evening clouds withdrawn, pure cold air floods the sky;

The River of Stars mute, a jade plate turns on high.

How oft can we enjoy a fine mid-autumn night?

Where shall we view next year a silver moon so bright?

浣溪沙·徐门石潭谢雨[①]，道上作五首

一

照日深红暖见鱼，
连村绿暗晚藏乌。
黄童[②]白叟[③]聚睢盱[④]。

麋鹿[⑤]逢人虽未惯，
猿猱[⑥]闻鼓不须呼。
归来说与采桑姑。

① 谢雨：旱后喜雨，设祭谢神。
② 黄童：黄发儿童。
③ 白叟：白发老人。
④ 睢（suī）盱（xū）：喜悦的样子。
⑤ 麋鹿：鹿类的一种。
⑥ 猿猱（náo）：猿类的一种。

第一首词写石潭周围的村野风光和谢雨时的欢乐热闹情景。全篇紧扣"谢雨"来写。上片写红日照彻深潭，水中游鱼活泼，连村树林深绿，乌鸦欢乐啼鸣，聚观谢雨的儿童和老人喜笑颜开，洋溢着词人与村民们的喜雨之情。下片写麋鹿和猿猱以不同的性格神态与人群安然相处，表现山乡的淳朴风俗，更衬托出谢雨场景的欢乐气氛。结尾再虚写回到家把见到的一切告诉"采桑姑"，深化喜雨之情，含而不露，耐人寻味。

Silk-washing Stream
Thanks for Rain at Stony Pool

I

In warm sunlight the Pool turns red where fish can be seen,
And trees can shelter crows at dusk with shades dark green.
With eyes wide open, old and young come out to see me.

Like deer the kids are not accustomed strangers to meet;
Like monkeys they appear unbidden as drums beat.
Back, they tell sisters picking leaves of mulberry.

二

旋[7]抹红妆看使君[8],
三三五五棘篱[9]门。
相排踏破茜[10]罗裙。

老幼扶携收麦社[11],
乌鸢[12]翔舞赛神村。
道逢醉叟卧黄昏。

三

麻叶层层檾[13]叶光,
谁家煮茧一村香?
隔篱娇语络丝娘[14]。

垂白杖藜抬醉眼,
捋青[15]捣麨[16]软饥肠。
问言豆叶几时黄?

[7] 旋:立即。
[8] 使君:词人自称。
[9] 棘篱:用荆条围成的篱笆。
[10] 茜:红色。
[11] 收麦社:收麦子后举行的祭神活动。
[12] 乌鸢:乌鸦和老鹰。
[13] 檾(qǐng):同"苘",俗称青麻。
[14] 络丝娘:本为虫名,此处代指缫丝的妇女。
[15] 捋青:从麦穗上捋下麦粒。青,新麦。
[16] 麨(chǎo):用麦子制成的食物。

第二首上片写农村姑娘拥拥挤挤看州官的情景,惟妙惟肖地表现了她们高兴、迫切、好奇、害羞的神态、动作、心理。下片写农村的迎神赛会,只勾勒了满村农民扶老携幼踊跃赴会和乌鸢盘旋低飞不去的两个细节,已显示出庆祝丰收的欢腾景象和迎神祭品的丰盛。结尾推出醉翁卧黄昏一个特写镜头,生动地表明祭神活动持续了一天,人们直到傍晚才尽欢而散。

II

Maidens make up in haste to see the magistrate;

By threes and fives they come out at their hedgerow gate.

They push and squeeze and trample each other's skirt red.

Villagers old and young to celebration are led;

With crows and kites they dance thanksgiving in array.

At dusk I see an old man lie drunk on my way.

III

The leaves of jute and hemp are thick and lush in this land;

The scent of boiling cocoons in the village spreads.

Across the fence young maidens prate while reeling threads.

An old man raises dim-sighted eyes, cane in hand;

He picks new wheat so that his hunger he may ease.

I wonder when will yellow the leaves of green peas.

  第三首：麻叶长得繁茂又光滑滋润，进入村庄，到处弥漫煮茧的香气，篱笆后的"娇语"是缫丝女的笑谈，还是纺织娘的夜吟？视觉、嗅觉、听觉，让求雨得雨的词人心生喜悦。然而，忽其笔锋一转，写老农醉眼迷离捣麦充饥的画面，与豆叶未黄的焦灼一问，撕开了丰收表象下的苦涩。苏轼以"捋青捣䴳"的触感直抵民生肌理，身为徐州太守的他，听见的不是风雅丝竹，而是饥饿肠胃与土地博弈的窘宰。

四

簌簌衣巾落枣花,
村南村北响缫车[17]。
牛衣古柳卖黄瓜。

酒困路长惟欲睡,
日高人渴漫思茶。
敲门试问野人家。

[17]缫(sāo)车:纺车。

第四首:枣花坠落的簌簌声,缫车转动的吱呀声,古柳下小贩的叫卖声,构成初夏乡村的三重奏。在此,苏轼以耳代目,让声音成为画面的经纬,借通感妙笔,勾勒出乡村生活的质朴模样。"敲门试问"四字尤妙,农家是否有人、能否喝上茶水都不再叙述。词虽止却给人留下了无穷的想象与韵味。同时,士大夫的矜持架子悄然碎落,官民之间原本森严的壁垒,也被一碗茶水轻易化解,尽显与民亲近的质朴情怀。

IV

Date flowers fall in showers on my hooded head;

At both ends of the village wheels are spinning thread;

A straw-cloaked man sells cucumbers 'neath a willow tree.

Wine-drowsy when the road is long, I yearn for bed;

Throat parched when the sun is high, I long for tea.

I knock at farmer's door to see to what he'll treat me.

五

软草平莎[18]过雨新,
轻沙走马路无尘。
何时收拾耦耕[19]身?

日暖桑麻光似泼,
风来蒿艾气如薰。
使君元[20]是此中人。

[18] 莎(suō):莎草。草本植物,可供药用。
[19] 耦(ǒu)耕:两人并耕。
[20] 元:通"原"。

第五首:莎草浸润雨水的绵软触感,马蹄奔走无尘沙路的清新环境,让苏轼发出"何时收拾耦耕身"的喟叹。日光暖暖,桑麻泛着光泽,熏风裹挟着蒿艾的气息。无限的温馨,袭人的芳香,似在质问宦海沉浮的意义。"使君元是此中人",词人深深感叹,他不再是路过乡村的观察者,而是重归土地的生命本体。这场谢雨之行,最终成了苏轼与乡土灵魂的重逢。

V

After rain the paddy fields look fresh as soft grass;

No dust is raised on sandy roads where horses pass.

When can I come to till the ground with household mine?

Hemp and mulberry glint as if steeped in sunshine;

Mugwort and moxa spread a sweet scent in the breeze.

I remember I was companion of all these.

浣溪沙

山色横侵①蘸晕霞②,
湘川风静吐寒花。
远林屋散尚啼鸦。

梦到故园多少路?
酒醒南望隔天涯。
月明千里照平沙③。

①横侵:纵横扩展。
②晕霞:指晚霞。
③平沙:广阔的沙原。

  晚霞如晕染,山色若侵云,深秋风静,寒花默开,远望屋宇炊烟,倦鸟归巢,是一幅氤氲墨韵的写意山水,也是一幅惹人相思的故园秋景。

  念家乡,醉梦回,酒醒方知隔天涯;唯有明月,照见千里,故乡故人共此月色。东坡有这样的妙笔巧思,把个人的思念扩展到往古来今、天宇地极,思念长而辽阔,不怨不伤,淡极而悠长!

Silk-washing Stream

The sky is barred with mountains steeped in flushing cloud;
The windless Southern Stream exhales cold blossoms proud;
Cottages in far-off woods with crying crows are still loud.

How far away in dreams, oh! is my native land!
Awake from wine, I find sky-scraping mountains stand;
For miles and miles the moon shines on the plain of sand.

浣溪沙

风压轻云贴水飞,
乍晴池馆燕争泥①。
沈郎②多病不胜衣。

沙上不闻鸿雁信③,
竹间时听鹧鸪啼。
此情惟有落花知。

① 燕争泥:燕子衔泥筑巢。
② 沈郎:即沈约,南朝梁诗人。
③ 鸿雁信:鸿雁传书。

  雨后微风轻拂、淡云贴水、春燕啄泥,满目生机盎然。然作者笔锋一转,自比多病的沈约,已然日渐消瘦,弱不胜衣。东坡惯用此种对比,从欣欣然到柔弱自怜情绪急转。此刻眼前所见沙洲上歇脚的鸟儿,也成了不传书的鸿雁,竹间鸟鸣也成了鹧鸪鸟"行不得也哥哥"的哀啼。春景无限,却是满怀凄苦无人诉,雨后落花成知己!
  思念是人生无法避开的劫,一念相思,满心凄凉!

Silk-washing Stream

Pressed by the breeze, over water the light clouds fly;
In pecking clods by poolside tower swallows vie.
I feel too weak to wear my gown, ill for so long.

I have not heard the message-bearing wild geese's song;
Partridges among bamboos seem to call me go home;
Only fallen blooms know the heart of those who roam.

浣溪沙·咏橘

菊暗荷枯一夜霜[1],
新苞[2]绿叶照林光。
竹篱茅舍出青黄。

香雾噀[3]人惊半破[4],
清泉[5]流齿怯初尝。
吴姬[6]三日手犹香。

[1] 一夜霜:橘子经霜之后,颜色变黄,味道也更鲜美。
[2] 新苞:指新橘。
[3] 噀(xùn):喷。
[4] 半破:刚刚剥开橘皮。
[5] 清泉:指橘子的汁液。
[6] 吴姬:吴地的女子。

　　一夜秋霜,菊残荷枯,新橘却泛出金黄的光,越发成熟了;繁茂的绿叶与青黄的果实间隐约现出竹篱茅舍,一"出"字,将农人辛勤和新橘初成联系起来,绝妙!

　　李白诗中的压酒吴姬,素手破吴橘。一"惊"一"怯",生动活泼,"惊"是破橘时油腺崩开,霏霏香雾直扑人面;"怯"是橘汁流淌齿间既酸且冷,未免面容瑟缩。读此句,仿佛新橘在手,酸甜之意自齿间袭至舌尖。

　　今之眉山亦多种橘树,漫山绵延的果林间偶现农家小院,恰似千年未变之景,坡公仙魂当知!

Silk-washing Stream
The Tangerine

After one night of frost

Chrysanthemums are darkened and lotus flowers lost.

The wood is brightened by leaves green and buds new,

The thatched cot and fence would grow yellow and blue.

Her mouth half open, she smells the fragrance sweet;

She's timid to drink the fountain her teeth meet.

Her hand still fragrant stays for three long days.

永遇乐

彭城①夜宿燕子楼,梦盼盼,因作此词。

明月如霜,
好风如水,
清景无限。
曲港跳鱼,
圆荷泻露,
寂寞无人见。
紞如②三鼓,
铿然③一叶,
黯黯梦云惊断。
夜茫茫,
重寻无处,
觉来小园行遍。

①彭城:今江苏省徐州市。
②紞(dǎn)如:击鼓声。
③铿(kēng)然:清脆的音响。

这首词上片写梦中所见燕子楼之景,开篇两句比喻活现出月之皎洁,风之清凉。接着写鱼跳露泻,一叶坠落竟有惊心的铿然之声,以动写静,以声衬寂。本是梦境,却如幻如真。又写梦醒后低回彷徨,可见心事之迷离低沉。下片将仕

Joy of Eternal Union
The Pavilion of Swallows

I lodged at the Pavilion of Swallows in Pengcheng, dreamed of the fair lady Panpan, and wrote the following poem.

The bright moonlight is like frost white,

The gentle breeze like water clean:

Far and wide extends the night scene.

In the haven fish leap

And dew-drops roll down lotus leaves

In solitude no man perceives.

Drums beat thrice in the night so deep,

A leaf falls with a tinkling sound so loud

That gloomy, I awake from my dream of the Cloud.

Under the boundless pall of night,

Nowhere again can she be found

Though in the small garden I have walked around.

宦的倦怀与燕子楼空人渺茫之眼前事比照，发出人生如寄、古今如梦的感慨。整首词叙事、议论与抒情浑然一体，笔调空灵，意境清幽深远。

天涯倦客,
山中归路,
望断故园心眼④。
燕子楼空,
佳人何在?
空锁楼中燕。
古今如梦,
何曾梦觉?
但有旧欢新怨。
异时对、黄楼⑤夜景,
为余浩叹!

④心眼:心愿。
⑤黄楼:徐州东门上的大楼,苏轼任徐州知州时所建。

A tired wayfarer far from home.

In the mountains may roam,

His native land from view is blocked.

The Pavilion of Swallows is empty.

Where is the lady so fair?

In the Pavilion only swallows' nest is locked.

Both the past and the present are like dreams,

From which we have ne'er been awake, it seems.

We have but joys and sorrows old and new.

Some other day others will come to view

The Yellow Tower's night scenery,

Then they would sigh for me!

续丽人行

李仲谋家有周昉画背面欠伸内人,极精,戏作此诗。

深宫无人春日长,
沉香亭北百花香。
美人睡起薄梳洗,
燕舞莺啼空断肠。
画工欲画无穷意,
背立东风初破睡[①]。
若教回首却嫣然,
阳城下蔡俱风靡。
杜陵饥客[②]眼长寒,
蹇驴破帽随金鞍。

① 初破睡:刚刚睡醒。
② 杜陵饥客:指杜甫。

这首题画诗立意构思独出心裁,别开生面。东坡认为画家绘背面美人,诱人想象,有无穷意味。然而"背面欠伸"的形象对于未见原画的读者来说,未免空虚。因此东坡在描绘了美人"背立东风初破睡"的意态后,又展现她"回首却嫣然"的镜头,将相对静止的画面形象化作动态的形象。又

Song of a Fair Lady

I saw an excellent picture drawn by Zhou Fang of a yawning lady singer viewed from the back, and I wrote this poem in joke as a companion poem of Du Fu's.

In the lonely deep palace the spring days were long.
North of the Fragrance Pavilion flowers smelt sweet.
The lightly-dressed fair lady got up at the song
Of orioles, her heart broke to see swallows fleet.
The painter tried to retain her infinite charm
And paint'd her back when, awake, she stood in the east wind.
If she turned her head with a smile, she would disarm
A besieging army, however disciplined.
The hungry poet Du Fu with a longing eye,
In shabby hat and on lame ass, followed a horse.

与随后想象杜甫在写《丽人行》时隔花临水偶见丽人背影的情景一起，照应题序所谓"背面欠伸内人"的画面。末两句以普通人家夫妻相敬如宾反衬宫女生活的孤寂苦闷。

隔花临水时一见,
只许腰肢背后看。
心醉归来茅屋底,
方信人间有西子。
君不见孟光③举案与眉齐,
何曾背面伤春啼!

③孟光:东汉贤士梁鸿之妻。每次孟光给梁鸿送饭时,把托盘举得跟眉毛一样高,夫妻十分恩爱。

Sometime across the flowery stream he passed by,

He saw but from the back her slender waist and torse.

Fascinated, he came back to his thatched cot,

And then believed on earth there was a lady fair.

Don't you know man and wife were happy with their lot?

Why should she turn her back and weep with a love-sick air?

除夜大雪，留潍州，元日早晴，遂行，中途雪复作

除夜雪相留，
元日晴相送。
东风吹宿酒，
瘦马兀①残梦。
葱昽晓光开，
旋转馀花弄。
下马成野酌，
佳哉谁与共！
须臾晚云合，
乱洒无缺空。

①兀：昏沉的样子。

　　除夕以雪佐酒，东风吹酒醒，骑着瘦马赶路，头脑昏沉，然见路边花开，瞬间脑清目明兴致大起，翻身下马，对花野酌，美哉美哉！不料天色忽变，大雪漫天，马身上挂满了鹅毛大雪，嘻！倒像是骑了一只雪白的凤凰。

　　潇洒恣意是东坡的常态！

　　此时为熙宁十年大年初一，东坡路过潍州。大雪漫山，行路颇难，然三年之旱黎民之伤，这一场瑞雪来得好啊！

Snow on New Year's Day

I was detained by a heavy snow at Weizhou on New Year's Eve, but on the morning of the first day it cleared and I resumed my journey. Along the way, it started to snow again.

Detained by snow on New Year's Eve,
On fine New Year's Day I take leave.
The east wind sobers me, though drunk deep,
My lean horse jerks me out of sleep,
Faintly and softly the day breaks,
From branches whirl down last snowflakes.
I dismount afield to take wine,
But none partake my drink divine.
Suddenly dark clouds gather quick,
And heavy snow falls fast and thick.

鹅毛垂马鬃,
自怪骑白凤。
三年东方旱,
逃户连敧栋②;
老农释耒③叹,
泪入饥肠痛。
春雪虽云晚,
春麦犹可种。
敢怨行役劳,
助尔歌饭瓮。

② 敧(qī)栋：破败的房屋。
③ 耒(lěi)：古代的一种农具，形状像木叉。

Like goose feathers it hangs down my horse's mane.

Am I on a phoenix without stain?

For three years the east saw drought rage

And the poor desert their village.

A peasant lays aside his plow and sighs,

His starving guts ache with tears from his eyes.

Although spring snow comes rather late,

Wheat can be sown at any rate.

Of hard journey can I complain?

——I write this to allay your pain.

李思训①画长江绝岛图

山苍苍,
水茫茫,
大孤小孤②江中央。
崖崩路绝猿鸟去,
惟有乔木搀③天长。
客舟何处来?
棹歌④中流声抑扬。
沙平风软望不到,
孤山久与船低昂。

①李思训:唐代著名画家。
②大孤小孤:指大孤山、小孤山。大孤山在今江西九江鄱阳湖中,小孤山在今安徽宿松东南长江中。
③搀:直刺。
④棹歌:划船人唱的歌。

　　东坡深得诗、画之趣,此诗诗画难辨,诗即是画,画即是诗。山水苍茫,画面空阔,显见得是一幅平远山水。江中山立,云烟袅袅,不见鸟迹猿踪,唯见乔木参天。客舟棹歌打破孤寂,山间回音相和,山如美人鬟、水若镜,临镜梳妆,贾客高声轻漫。莫轻狂呀,小孤山已然名花有主,嫁与彭浪矶啦!由画成诗,从静到动。画中本无猿鸟,东坡却说"猿

Two Lonely Isles in the Yangzi River
—Written on a Picture Drawn by Li Sixun

Below the mountains green

Water runs till unseen;

In the midst of the stream two lonely isles stand high.

Fallen crags bar the way;

Birds and apes cannot stay;

Only the giant trees tower into the sky.

From where comes a sail white?

In mid-stream rises oarsmen's undulating song.

Sand bar is flat, the wind is weak, no boat in sight,

The Lonely Isles sink and swim with the sail for long,

鸟绝",引人遐想云烟之下乔木之间鸟兽奔行。客舟一叶,却说"棹歌""贾客轻狂",小孤山是"小姑",彭浪矶是"彭郎",巧用当地"彭郎是小姑夫婿"的传说,跳脱妙思、"神完气足、遒转空妙"!

峨峨两烟鬟,
晓镜开新妆。
舟中贾客莫漫狂,
小姑⑤前年嫁彭郎⑥。

⑤小姑:指小孤山。
⑥彭郎:即彭浪矶。

Like mist-veiled tresses of a pretty lass

Using the river as her looking glass.

O merchant in the boat, don't go mad for the fair!

The Lonely Isle and Gallant Hill are a well-matched pair.

百步洪[①]（二首选一）

长洪斗落生跳波，
轻舟南下如投梭[②]。
水师[③]绝叫凫雁[④]起，
乱石一线争磋磨。
有如兔走鹰隼落，
骏马下注千丈坡。
断弦离柱箭脱手，
飞电过隙珠翻荷。
四山眩转风掠耳，
但见流沫生千涡。
崄中得乐虽一快，
何异水伯夸秋河[⑤]。

① 百步洪：泗水的一处急流，在今江苏省徐州市东南。
② 投梭：形容舟行之快，如织布之梭。
③ 水师：船工。
④ 凫雁：野鸭子。
⑤ 水伯夸秋河：典出《庄子·秋水》。水伯指黄河之神河伯，秋河指秋季的黄河，夸：炫耀。传说秋季黄河水量充沛，河伯见自身水域浩大，便骄傲地以为天下之美尽在己身，后顺流东行见到无边无际的海洋，方知自身渺小，始悟大道。

诗分两半，前观激流，后悟人生。

百步洪水湍急抖落、轻舟疾若飞梭，水手惊呼、岸边凫雁惊飞、水拍乱石，读诗人亦未免与舟中人一起紧张。接着以狡兔疾走、鹰隼猛落、骏马飞奔、断弦离柱、飞箭离弦、飞电过隙、荷叶流珠这种连篇累叠的比喻来形容水流之急、猛，激湍奔腾、声势壮阔如耳闻目见，渲染入神，直令人

The Hundred-pace Rapids

Leaping waves grow where the long rapids steeply fall,

A light boat shoots south like a plunging shuttle. Lo!

Waterbirds fly up at the boatman's desperate call.

Among jagged rocks it strives to thread its way and go

As a hare darts away, an eagle dives below,

A gallant steed gallops down a slope beyond control,

A string snaps from a lute, an arrow from a bow,

Lightning cleaves clouds or off lotus leaves raindrops roll.

The mountains whirl around, the wind sweeps by the ear,

I see the current boil in a thousand whirlpools.

At the risk of life I feel a joy without peer,

Unlike the god who boasts of the river he rules.

神往！

  历大奇险有大快意，然诗人的笔迅速从如泼墨般的洒脱恣意到言事理的谨慎。人生、名利皆如逝水，有其时空限度，物是人非是常态。人的思绪却可穿越往古来今天宇地极，故不受造物所限。"乘化"是道家哲思，"逾新罗""住""劫"是佛家语。由长洪激流到逝水再到佛道，诗家成了思想家。

我生乘化⑥日夜逝,
坐觉一念逾新罗⑦。
纷纷争夺醉梦里,
岂信荆棘埋铜驼。
觉来俯仰失千劫⑧,
回视此水殊委蛇⑨。
君看岸边苍石上,
古来篙眼如蜂窠。
但应此心无所住,
造物虽驶如吾何!
回船上马各归去,
多言哓哓⑩师所呵。

⑥乘化:顺应自然。
⑦新罗:朝鲜半岛古国名。
⑧千劫:犹言时间之长。
⑨委蛇(wēi yí):曲折行进的样子。
⑩哓哓(xiāo):说个不停。

I give in to changes that take place day and night,
My thoughts can wander far away though I sit here.
Many people in drunken dreams contend and fight.
Do they know palaces 'mid weeds will disappear?
Awakened, they'd regret to have lost a thousand days;
Coming here, they will find the river freely rolls.
If on the riverside rocks you just turn your gaze,
You will see they are honeycombed by the punt-poles.
If your mind from earthly things is detached and freed,
Although nature may change, you'll never be care-worn.
Let us go back or in a boat or on a steed.
Our Abbot will hold this vain argument in scorn.

舟中夜起

微风萧萧吹菰蒲①,
开门看雨月满湖。
舟人水鸟两同梦,
大鱼惊窜如奔狐。
夜深人物不相管,
我独形影相嬉娱。
暗潮生渚②吊③寒蚓④,
落月挂柳看悬蛛。
此生忽忽⑤忧患里,
清境过眼能须臾⑥!
鸡鸣钟动百鸟散,
船头击鼓还相呼。

①菰(gū)蒲:茭白和菖蒲。
②渚:水边。
③吊:怜悯。
④寒蚓:蚯蚓。
⑤忽忽:恍惚的样子。
⑥能须臾:如此快。

    风声似雨声,推门看雨却惊见月色满湖,夜色空明、静谧奇幻。月明如昼,鱼惊若狐,一动更生一静,以鱼喻狐狸,思路有趣,不觉一笑。蚯蚓、蜘蛛皆入诗,却有暗潮生渚、落月挂柳相配,故而不减其美,真奇逸之句!

    东坡喜夜中独赏天地之美,静夜自娱、物我同一。"独"

Getting up at Night While in a Boat

I take for rain the breeze which rustles through the reed,

Opening the hatch, I find a lake full of moonbeams.

Boatmen and waterbirds share alike the same dreams;

Like scurrying foxes, startled fish away speed.

Man and nature forget each other when night is deep,

Playing alone with my shadow amuses me.

The setting moon like spider hangs from willow tree;

Dark tides creeping over the flats for earthworms weep.

Our life laden with care and spent in worry fleets,

A pure vision before the eyes cannot last long.

Flocks of birds scatter at ringing bells and cock's song,

You'll hear from the prow but boatmen's shout and drumbeats.

是独赏满湖月色，也是廿载许国如独行；忧患长久，清静须臾，鸡鸣之后，眼前又是纷扰仕途。

　　传统文人往往许国之志与清静超然之心相悖，两两相济而不忘，方是东坡！

陈季常①所蓄朱陈村嫁娶图二首

一

何年顾陆②丹青手，
画作朱陈嫁娶图。
闻道一村惟两姓，
不将门户买崔卢③。

二

我是朱陈旧使君④，
劝农曾入杏花村。
而今风物那堪画，
县吏催钱夜打门。

①陈季常：名慥，字季常，四川眉山人，北宋隐士。
②顾陆：顾恺之、陆探微，均是六朝时著名画家。
③崔卢：崔姓、卢姓，泛指名门大族。
④使君：唐宋时对太守的别称。

  这是东坡为陈季常所藏画而作的两首题画诗。《朱陈村嫁娶图》为五代时前蜀人赵德元根据白居易《朱陈村诗》的内容绘成，表现了朱陈村人安居乐业、嫁娶不讲门第、没有贫贱悬隔等淳朴敦厚的民俗。第一首写朱陈村美好的过去，第二首写朱陈村现在的情况，两首诗前后形成鲜明对比，表现出诗人对当下现实的愤慨之情。两首诗语言质朴，却有极强的感情色彩。

A Picture of Wedding in Zhu-Chen Village

I

A great master of ancient days like Gu or Lu

Painted this picture of wedding of Chen and Zhu.

'Tis said the villagers bear only these two names,

They would not change their household for Cui's and Lu's fames.

II

I came among apricot trees to advocate

Farming in their village when I was magistrate.

But now you can find such picturesque scene no more,

For tax-collectors will nightly knock at the door.

湖州

小园幽榭枕苹汀

南歌子·湖州作

山雨潇潇过,
溪桥浏浏①清。
小园幽榭枕苹汀。
门外月华如水、
彩舟横。

苕②岸霜花尽,
江湖雪阵平。
两山遥指海门青。
回首水云何处、
觅孤城?

①浏浏:水流清澈的样子。
②苕(tiáo):芦苇的花。

  山雨潇潇过,小桥流水清,园中水榭似枕在浮萍之上。雨后月色若水,溪桥下小舟横卧,这彩舟既承载了端午的热闹,又寓意着友人的别离。
  岸边若白霜铺陈的芦花已尽,江中如雪的浪涛渐平。夜色中两山相隔,海门在望,友人乘船将去,回首时,唯见寂寥之人、孤独之城。
  词作于元丰二年(1079)五月,于湖州钱氏园送刘挚。于澄明夜色中抒发离愁,清新雅致,末尾写友人离别回望,离人与归人共此离愁别绪,别具巧思。

A Southern Song
Written at Lakeside County

Shower on shower passes o'er the hills,

Clear, clear water flows 'neath bridges in the rills.

A garden pillows its bower amid the weed.

Outdoors in liquid moonlight lies afloat

A painted boat.

Frost cleared away on rivershore,

By waterside snow lingering no more.

Afar stands the blue gate to which two mountains lead.

Looking back, I find cloud and water up and down.

Where is the lonely town?

端午遍游诸寺得禅字

肩舆①任所适,
遇胜②辄③流连。
焚香引幽步,
酌茗开净筵④。
微雨止还作,
小窗幽更妍。
盆山不见日,
草木自苍然。
忽登最高塔⑤,
眼界穷大千。
卞峰照城郭,
震泽⑥浮云天。

①肩舆:一种用人力抬扛的代步工具,在两根竹竿中间设软椅以坐人。
②胜:美景。
③辄:就。
④净筵:素斋。
⑤最高塔:指湖州飞英寺中的飞英塔。
⑥震泽:太湖。

这首纪游诗,写优哉游哉的一日所游,先写焚香探幽,品茶吃素,继而写寺院及四围景色,再写登上飞英塔所见卞山、城郭、太湖之景。最后写游兴未毕,却已是炊烟四起,入夜仍没有睡意,可见作者游兴之浓,对湖州山光水色之热爱。诗中用字极见功力,如用一个"浮"字写太湖的气势,一个"造"字写微雨渐止后、夕阳斜照、城郭明灭的情景,极为准确、生动传神。

Visiting Temples on the Dragon Boat Festival

I go sight-seeing in my sedan-chair
And stop where there's a scenic spot to see.
Burning incense attracts me to go where
I may have vegetable feast and tea.
The gentle rain stops and then starts again,
The little window looks gloomy and clean.
Shut out from sunlight by the hills, the plain
Is overspread with grass and trees so green.
When I ascend the peak'd pagoda, all
The boundless land extends before my eyes.
The Northern Peak o'erlooks the city wall;
On the Lake Zhenze float the cloudy skies.

深沉既可喜,
旷荡⑦亦所便。
幽寻未云毕,
墟落⑧生晚烟。
归来记所历,
耿耿⑨清不眠。
道人⑩亦未寝,
孤灯同夜禅。

⑦旷荡:旷达。
⑧墟落:村落。
⑨耿耿:有心事的样子。
⑩道人:指僧人道潜,苏轼的好友。

A quiet place affords me keen delight;
In space immense I feel under no yoke.
Still looking for some more secluded sight,
I see from villages rise evening smoke.
Come back, I write down my impression deep,
Musing o'er it, I pass a sleepless night.
Nor do the devoted monks take their sleep,
They sit in meditation by lamplight.

黄州

世事一场大梦

雨晴后,步至四望亭①下渔池上,遂自乾明寺前东冈上归二首

一

雨过浮萍合,
蛙声满四邻。
海棠真一梦,
梅子欲尝新。
拄杖闲挑菜,
秋千不见人。
殷勤木芍药②,
独自殿③余春。

二

高亭废已久,
下有种鱼塘。

①四望亭:在今湖北省黄冈市。
②木芍药:牡丹花的别称。
③殿:原指行军走在队伍最后,后泛指序列之末。

　　苏轼被贬黄州,常独自一人钓鱼采药以自娱,信步逍遥以自适,二诗即这种生活的写照。第一首诗写春末夏初雨后天晴散步所见之景。诗中用梦来形容海棠花的凋谢,浸透了诗人此时独有的感受,被贬黄州何尝不是一场噩梦。又以牡丹花独自在暮春开放,反衬百花凋零,春光已失。诗人借物

The Four-view Pavilion

I

Duckweeds meet after the showers,

Frogs are croaking far and near.

Like dreams fade crab-apple flowers,

Yet we may taste fresh plums here.

I carry vegetables, cane in hand,

And see no maiden on the swing.

But pleasing peonies there stand,

Alone they crown departing spring.

II

The high pavilion lies ruined for long,

But below there still remains a fish pond.

抒情,借对海棠生命短暂,表达对春天易逝的惜春伤春之情,借对牡丹花的赞扬,表达自己虽被贬谪,孤寂感伤,依然要坚守自我的心志。第二首诗亦是景中见人,以景衬人,从中亦可分明地感受到诗人的孤寂、孤清心境。

暮色千山人,
春风百草香。
市桥人寂寂,
古寺竹苍苍。
鹳鹤来何处?
号鸣满夕阳!

In the dusk a thousand hills are drowned;

The spring breeze is sweet with herbs in throng.

The market place appears forlorn;

The old temple with bamboo is green.

Stork and crane come to enliven the scene,

The setting sun is o'erflowed with their horn.

西江月·黄州中秋

世事一场大梦，
人生几度秋凉。
夜来风叶已鸣廊，
看取眉头鬓上。

酒贱常愁客少，
月明多被云妨①。
中秋谁与共孤光？
把盏凄然北望。

①妨：遮蔽。

    这首词反映东坡谪居后的苦闷心情，基调低沉哀婉。上片落笔便喟叹世事如梦、人生短促，接着写昨夜风吹落叶之声响于长廊，自己凄然顾影，但见鬓发斑斑。下片借酒贱客少委婉地点出词人遭贬斥后他人避之如水火的情形，又以浮云蔽月隐喻奸人当道，自己因谗遭贬，表达了对亲人的思念，对群小当道的愤懑，以及渴望被朝廷重用的深沉情感。整首词将吟咏节令与感慨身世、抒发悲情紧密结合，以景寓情，情景交融，意蕴丰厚，读来悲凉彻骨。

The Moon on the West River

Like dreams pass world affairs untold,
How many autumns in our life are cold?
My corridor is loud with wind-blown leaves at night.
See my brows frown and hair turn white!

Of my poor wine few guests are proud;
The bright moon is oft veiled in cloud.
Who would enjoy with me the mid-autumn moon lonely?
Wine cup in hand, northward I look only.

西江月

顷在黄州,春夜行蕲水①中,过酒家饮;酒醉,乘月至一溪桥上,解鞍曲肱,醉卧,少休;及觉,已晓,乱山攒拥,流水锵然,疑非尘世也。书此语桥柱上。

照野弥弥②浅浪,
横空隐隐层霄③。
障泥④未解玉骢骄⑤,
我欲醉眠芳草。

可惜⑥一溪风月,
莫教踏碎琼瑶⑦。
解鞍欹枕⑧绿杨桥,
杜宇⑨一声春晓。

①蕲(qí)水:水名,在黄州附近。
②弥(mǐ)弥:水波荡漾的样子。
③层霄:弥漫的云气。
④障泥:马鞯,垂于马两侧用于遮挡泥土。
⑤骄:健壮的样子。
⑥可惜:可爱。
⑦琼瑶:指月亮在水中的倒影。
⑧欹枕:斜倚枕头之意。
⑨杜宇:杜鹃鸟。

浅浪、层霄、芳草、风月、琼瑶、绿杨、春晓,一句一景;风、云、水、月、溪、桥融为一体,幽美静谧,洗净风尘,洁若仙境。然细看诗题,不过乱山流水荒野一色,入东坡青眼,竟是仙境!非景若仙境,是心若仙心、人若仙人也!

The Moon on the West River
Lines Written on a Bridge

Wave on wave glimmers by the river shores;

Sphere on sphere dimly appears in the sky

Though unsaddled is my white-jade-like horse,

Drunken, asleep in the sweet grass I'll lie.

My horse's hoofs may break, I'm afraid,

The breeze-rippled brook paved by the moon with white jade.

I tether my horse to a green willow

On the bridge and I pillow

My head on my arm till the cuckoo's songs awake

A spring daybreak.

定风波

三月七日,沙湖道中遇雨,雨具先去,同行皆狼狈,余独不觉。已而①遂晴,故作此。

莫听穿林打叶声。
何妨吟啸且徐行。
竹杖芒鞋②轻胜马,
谁怕!
一蓑烟雨任平生。

①已而:过了一会儿。
②芒鞋:草鞋。

东坡一生在政治上之遭遇,极为波动,时而内召,时而外用,时而位置清要之地,时而放逐于边远之地,然而思想行为不因此而有所改变,反而愈遭挫折,愈见刚强,挫折愈大,声誉愈高。此词写途中遇雨之事,所表现的在风雨中吟啸徐行、从容自如,正是东坡达观的人生态度与超旷的精神世界的体现,全词显出一种旷达飘逸之致。

Calming the Waves
Caught in Rain on My Way to the Sandy Lake

On the 7th day of the 3rd month we were caught in rain on our way to the Sandy Lake. The umbrellas had gone ahead, my companions were quite downhearted, but I took no notice. It soon cleared, and I wrote this.

Listen not to the rain beating against the trees.
I had better walk slowly while chanting at ease.
Better than a saddle I like sandals and cane.
I'd fain,
In a straw cloak, spend my life in mist and rain.

料峭③春风吹酒醒,
微冷。
山头斜照却相迎。
回首向来萧瑟处,
归去。
也无风雨也无晴。

③料峭:微寒。

Drunken, I am sobered by the vernal wind shrill

And rather chill.

In front, I see the slanting sun atop the hill;

Turning my head, I see the dreary beaten track.

Let me go back!

Impervious to rain or shine, I'll have my own will.

浣溪沙

游蕲水清泉寺,寺临兰溪,溪水西流。

山下兰芽短浸溪,
松间沙路净无泥。
萧萧①暮雨子规②啼。

谁道人生无再少?
门前流水尚能西。
休将白发唱黄鸡!

①萧萧:形容雨声。
②子规:杜鹃鸟。

苏轼贬谪黄州期间,曾前往沙湖购田,患上疾病,便去浠水聋医庞安常处治疗。病愈后,与庞同游清泉寺,作此词。上片写眼前景,兰芽短浸、沙路无泥、萧萧暮雨中传来杜鹃鸟的啼叫声,这清新明朗的景象,正反映出词人病愈后的喜悦心情。下片即景感慨,面对西流的兰溪,如同唱响了一曲意气风发的生命交响乐,表现出词人以顺处逆的豪迈情怀与积极乐观的人生态度,读之令人奋发自强。

Silk-washing Stream

Visit to the Temple of Clear Fountain on the West-flowing Stream of Orchid.

In the brook below the hill is drowned short orchid bud;
On the sandy path between pine-trees there's no mud.
Shower by shower falls the rain while cuckoos sing.

Who says a man cannot be restored to his spring?
In front of the temple the water still flows west.
Why can't the cock crow at dawn though with a white crest?

念奴娇·赤壁怀古

大江①东去,
浪淘尽,
千古风流人物。
故垒②西边,
人道是、三国周郎③赤壁。
乱石崩云,
惊涛拍岸,
卷起千堆雪④。
江山如画,
一时多少豪杰。

①大江:指长江。
②故垒:过去遗留下来的营垒。
③周郎:指三国时吴国名将周瑜,字公瑾。
④雪:喻浪花。

　　这首词上阕描绘赤壁的雄奇景色。开端从滚滚东流的长江着笔,布设了极广阔悠远的时空背景,把读者带入千古兴亡的历史氛围中。点明赤壁之后,大笔渲染乱石、惊涛、雪浪,惊心动魄,境界奇险,为英雄人物出场作了有力的铺垫。下阕借咏古代英杰抒情遣怀,抒写自己有志报国而壮志难酬的

The Charm of a Maiden Singer
The Red Cliff

The great river eastward flows;

With its waves are gone all those

Gallant heroes of bygone years.

West of the ancient fortress appears

Red Cliff where General Zhou won his early fame

When the Three Kingdoms were in flame.

Rocks tower in the air and waves beat on the shore.

Rolling up a thousand heaps of snow.

To match the land so fair, how many heroes of yore

Had made great show!

感慨,同时将自己对宇宙人生的思考置于其中,显示出他善以超然旷达的态度消解人生失意的逸怀浩气。全词起伏跌宕,笔力劲拔,气象雄奇壮阔,历来被公认为是东坡沉雄豪放风格的千古绝唱。

遥想公瑾当年,
小乔初嫁了,
雄姿英发。
羽扇⑤纶巾⑥,
谈笑间、樯橹⑦灰飞烟灭。
故国神游,
多情应笑我,
早生华发。
人间如梦,
一尊还酹江月。

⑤羽扇:羽毛制成的扇子。
⑥纶(guān)巾:青丝制成的头巾。
⑦樯橹:指曹操军队的战船。樯,桅杆;橹,船桨。

I fancy General Zhou at the height

Of his success, with a plume fan in hand,

In a silk hood, so brave and bright,

Laughing and jesting with his bride so fair,

While enemy ships were destroyed as planned

Like castles in the air.

Should their souls revisit this land,

Sentimental, his bride would laugh to say:

Younger than they, I have my hair turned grey.

Life is but like a dream.

O Moon, I drink to you who have seen them on the stream.

临江仙·夜归临皋

夜饮东坡[①](#)醒复醉,
归来仿佛三更。
家童鼻息已雷鸣。
敲门都不应,
倚杖听江声。

长恨此身非我有,
何时忘却营营[②](#)?
夜阑风静縠纹[③](#)平。
小舟从此逝,
江海寄余生。

① 东坡:在湖北省黄冈市东。
② 营营:指追求、奔逐。
③ 縠(hú)纹:水波细纹。

  这首词上片写醉归。先写纵饮的豪兴和醉眼蒙眬的情态,再从敲门不应、倚杖听涛的行为动作,写出他随遇而安的生活态度与达观超旷的精神世界。同时,以声衬静,借家童的鼾声、词人的敲门声以及江声的衬托,营造出一个安恬静美的秋夜境界。下片抒感慨。"长恨""何时"两句慨叹,表现了词人摆脱功名利禄羁束、追求精神自由超脱的心愿。接着以一个写景句,展现秋夜江天风平浪静、寥廓美好的景致,

Riverside Daffodils
Returning to Lingao by Night

Drinking at Eastern Slope by night,
I sober, then get drunk again.
When I come back, it seems to be mid-night.
I hear the thunder of my houseboy's snore,
I knock but none answers the door.
What can I do but, leaning on my cane,
Listen to the river's refrain?

I long regret I am not master of my own.
When can I ignore the hums of up and down?
In the still night the soft winds quiver
On the ripples of the river.
From now on, I would vanish with my little boat,
For the rest of my life, on the sea I would float.

活画出词人顾盼自如、欣然陶醉的神情意态，隐喻着词人对静谧空阔的理想天地的向往与追求。"小舟"二句承上表达了驾舟浪迹江海、将余生融入大自然的心音，也使全篇增添了飘逸浪漫的情调。

卜算子·黄州定慧院①寓居作

缺月挂疏桐,
漏断②人初静。
谁见幽人独往来?
缥缈孤鸿影。

惊起却回头,
有恨无人省。
拣尽寒枝不肯栖,
寂寞沙洲冷。

① 定慧院:在今湖北省黄冈市东南。苏轼被贬黄州时,曾于此居住。
② 漏断:指深夜。漏,古人计时用的漏壶。

东坡以戴罪之身来到黄州,虽得以脱离囹圄之苦、死生之忧,然其心境却通过此词展现了出来。上片点染出一幅凄清冷寂的月夜图景,凸显了一位独来独往、心事浩茫的幽人形象。下片细腻地描绘孤鸿的神情动态,正是词人刚出乌台惊魂未定、苦闷抑郁、顾影自怜的生动写照。作者以象征手法,托物寓意,通过孤鸿缥缈、惊起回头、怀抱幽恨和选求宿处,表达了自己虽身遭厄运却孤高自许、不愿随波逐流的情怀。全篇选景叙事简约凝练,含蓄蕴藉,笼罩着一层浓郁的孤独与感伤色调。

Song of Divination
Written at Dinghui Abbey in Huangzhou

From a sparse plane tree hangs the waning moon,
The waterclock is still and hushed is man.
Who sees a hermit pacing up and down alone?
Is it the shadow of a fugitive swan?

Startled, he turns his head
With a grief none behold.
Looking all over, he won't perch on branches dead
But on the lonely sandbank cold.

南乡子·重九①涵辉楼②呈徐君猷③

霜降水痕收④,
浅碧鳞鳞⑤露远洲。
酒力渐消风力软,
飕飕,
破帽多情却恋头。

佳节若为酬⑥,
但把清樽断送秋。
万事到头都是梦,
休休⑦,
明日黄花蝶也愁。

①重九:重阳节。
②涵辉楼:在黄州。
③徐君猷(yóu):时任黄州知州。
④水痕收:水位降低。
⑤鳞鳞:形容水波如鱼鳞一般。
⑥若为酬:怎样应付过去。
⑦休休:不要,这里指不要再提往事。

"万事到头都是梦,休休",与苏轼其他词中"人生如梦""世事一场大梦""未转头时皆梦"等慨叹异曲同工,语似自宽,实含一腔幽怨。在苏轼看来,世间万事皆是梦,荣辱得失、富贵贫贱都是过眼云烟,世间纷扰不必耿耿于怀。仕进则努力一展抱负,退则饮酒作乐终老余生,进取与退隐、积极与消极,失意却达观,这就是其时的苏轼。

Song of Southern Country
To Governor Xu on Mountain-climbing Day

The tide flows out after the fall of frost,

From rippling green water a beach of sand will rise.

The soughing wind softens, the vigor of wine is lost,

When blows the breeze,

My sympathetic hat won't leave my head with ease,

How shall we pass the holiday?

Wine cup in hand, we may send autumn away.

Everything will end in dreams,

It seems

Tomorrow fallen blooms will sadden butterflies.

鹧鸪天

林断山明竹隐墙。
乱蝉衰草小池塘。
翻空①白鸟时时见,
照水红蕖②细细香。

村舍外,古城傍。
杖藜徐步转斜阳。
殷勤昨夜三更雨,
又得浮生一日凉。

①翻空:飞在空中。
②红蕖(qú):荷花。

　　浮生若梦难得闲,但对于云端跌落贬谪黄州的苏轼来说,其身得闲其心亦得闲,这便不易了。上阕写景,"林断山明竹隐墙",山村远景高低错落、疏密明暗一语尽现;白鸟翻空、红蕖照水,有色有香有动态,勾画一幅清幽静美生气勃勃的江村之景。下阕叙事中流露闲怡之趣,一"转"一"殷勤",似乎心一闲万物便有情,其随遇而安、自得其乐的旷放之情跃然字里行间。

Partridges in the Sky
One More Fresh Day

Through forest breaks appear hills and bamboo-screened wall,
Cicadas shrill o'er withered grass near a pool small.
White birds are seen now and then looping in the air;
Pink lotus blooms on lake-side exude fragrance spare.

Beyond the cots,
Near the old town,
Cane in hand, I stroll round while the sun's slanting down.
Thanks to the welcome rain which fell when night was deep,
Now in my floating life one more fresh day I reap.

满庭芳

有王长官①者,弃官黄州三十三年,黄人谓之王先生。因送陈慥②来过③余,因为赋此。

三十三年,
今谁存者?
算只君与长江。
凛然苍桧④,
霜干苦难双。
闻道司州古县,
云溪上、竹坞⑤松窗。
江南岸,
不因送子⑥,
宁肯过吾邦?

① 王长官:苏轼好友,生迹不详。
② 陈慥(zào):字季常,苏轼好友。
③ 过:拜访。
④ 桧:圆柏。
⑤ 竹坞:用竹子建成的房屋。
⑥ 子:指陈慥。

知己相会,千杯空缸,实乃人生快事。其时苏轼被贬黄州,昔日朋友多有避忌,陈慥却一直与苏轼相从甚密,这次王长官送陈慥来会东坡,三人畅谈畅饮,岂不痛快!上片颂扬王长官高洁人品,发语便雄阔惊人,言其与长江一样饱经

Courtyard Full of Fragrance

After thirty-three years.

Who still remains today?

Only you and the long, long river stay.

Upright like the cypress evergreen,

Frost-proof, you have no compeers.

In your old county I have seen

Your cot surrounded by bamboos

Standing by cloudy stream framed with pine tree on tree.

If you leave the southern shore not to say adieus,

How could you come to see me?

沧桑；再以凛然苍桧与云溪竹松衬其孤高傲岸、正直耿介，一位不慕荣利、风神萧散的高士形象跃然纸上。下片描绘三人会饮时的情景。

摐摐⁷,
疏雨过,
风林舞破,
烟盖云幢。
愿持此邀君,
一饮空缸。
居士先生老矣,
真梦里、相对残釭。
歌声断,
行人未起,
船鼓已逢逢⁸。

⑦摐摐(chuāng):形容雨声。
⑧逢逢(páng):形容鼓声,此处指开船的信号。

After a sudden shower the trees

Dance in the breeze,

A veil of mist rises with cloud screen.

I hold high the wine cup

And invite you to drink it up.

Now old, I think it's like a dream sweet

To drink face to face with you.

We hear no more songs of adieu,

For early risers, drums begin to beat.

满庭芳

蜗角①虚名,
蝇头微利,
算来著甚干忙②?
事皆前定,
谁弱又谁强?
且趁闲身未老,
须放我、些子③疏狂!
百年里,
浑教是醉,
三万六千场。

①蜗角:蜗牛触角,和下一句的"蝇头",比喻极其微小。
②著甚干忙:白忙什么。著,同"着"。甚,什么;干忙,白忙。
③些子:一点儿。

把盏高歌,一曲悲慨诉衷肠,虚名浮利怎抵清风皓月、云幕高张!被贬黄州的苏轼对人生有了更清醒的审视:得失荣辱、祸福生死不可强求,无须说短论长,倒是身心与自然融为一体方能获得真正的自由。有失意的愤世嫉俗,更有大胸襟的飘逸旷达,给追名逐利者以棒喝,给恬淡自适者以慰藉,给现世浮躁者以自省。

Courtyard Full of Fragrance

For fame as vain as a snail's horn
And profit as slight as a fly's head,
Should I be busy and forlorn?
Fate rules for long,
Who is weak? Who is strong?
Not yet grown old and having leisure,
Let me be free to enjoy pleasure!
Could I be drunk in a hundred years,
Thirty-six hundred times without shedding tears?

思量,
能几许,
忧愁风雨,
一半相妨。
又何须,
抵死说短论长?
幸对清风皓月,
苔茵④展、云幕高张。
江南好,
千钟⑤美酒,
一曲满庭芳。

④苔茵:如褥的草地。
⑤钟:即"盅",酒器。

Think how long life can last,

Though sad and harmful storms I've passed.

Why should I waste my breath

Until my death,

To say the short and long

Or right and wrong?

I am happy to enjoy clear breeze and the moon bright,

Green grass outspread

And a canopy of cloud white.

The Southern shore is fine

With a thousand cups of wine

And the courtyard fragrant with song.

满庭芳·留别雪堂①

元丰七年四月一日,余将去黄移汝,留别雪堂邻里二三君子。会李仲览自江东来别,遂书以遗之。

归去来兮,
吾归何处?
万里家在岷峨②。
百年强半③,
来日苦无多。
坐见黄州再闰④,
儿童尽、吴语楚歌。
山中友,
鸡豚社酒,
相劝老东坡。

①雪堂:苏轼在黄州的住所,位于长江边上。
②岷(mín)峨(é):四川的岷山与峨眉山,此处代指作者故乡。
③强半:大半。
④再闰:阴历三年一闰,两闰为六年,作者自元丰二年贬至黄州,元丰三年闰九月,元丰六年闰六月,故称"再闰"。

元丰七年(1084)四月,谪居黄州的苏轼接到量移汝州的诰命。黄州,于苏轼而言是极其难言的,离别在即,更有万般滋味在心头。开篇"归去来兮,吾归何处?"借用陶渊明的《归去来辞》成句,抒发对故乡的深深思念;"儿童尽、楚语吴歌""山中友,鸡豚社酒,相劝老东坡",展现与黄州父老之间深厚的情谊,依依不舍之情溢于言表。下阕继而感叹时光易逝,来日无多,透露着一种淡淡的忧伤和无奈;然

Courtyard Full of Fragrance
Leaving My Hall of Snow

Why not go home?

Where shall I go today?

My home in Eyebrow Mountain is thousand miles away.

Fifty years old, I have not many days to come.

Living here for four years,

My children sing the Southern song.

Villagers and mountaineers

With meat and wine ask me to stay

In Eastern Slope for long.

而词人再一转,借"秋风""洛水"等自然景物,流露出对未来的期许和对宁静生活的向往。整首词言语质朴无华,却能字字打动人心,窥见一颗历经苦难之后忧伤而无怨愤、沧桑却不失希望的心。

云何?
当此去,
人生底事⑤,
来往如梭。
待闲看,
秋风洛水⑥清波。
好在堂前细柳,
应念我、莫剪柔柯⑦。
仍传语,
江南父老,
时与晒渔蓑!

⑤底事:何事。
⑥秋风洛水:西晋张翰在洛阳做官,见秋风起,思念故乡的菰菜、莼羹、鲈鱼脍,便弃官而归,此处表示退隐还乡之愿。
⑦柔柯:柳枝。

What shall I say

When I've left here?

How will my life appear?

Just as a shuttle comes and goes.

At leisure I'll see autumn breeze blows

And ripples the river clear,

I'll think of my willow tree slender.

Will you trim for me its twigs tender?

Please tell Southern villagers not to forget

To bask my straw cloak and fishing net!

虞美人

波声拍枕长淮①晓,
隙月②窥人小。
无情汴水③自东流,
只载一船离恨、向西州。

竹溪花浦曾同醉,
酒味多于泪。
谁教风鉴④在尘埃,
酝造一场烦恼、送人来!

①长淮:指淮河。
②隙月:从缝隙中透进的月光。
③汴水:古河名。
④风鉴:指风度见识。

  这首词是苏轼至高邮与友人秦观相会后,秦观一路送行至淮河,二人在河边饮别后所作。
  上阕写词人饮别秦观后乘船独往一夜难眠,只觉汴水无情流,满船离恨深;下阕回忆二人欢聚畅饮的情景,以冲淡离别的伤感,同时用玩笑般的口吻叹息秦观如此贤材被埋没,才能与自己相识,造成如今分别时的烦恼。全词由景入情,由自然引入人生,抒发词人人生短暂、壮志难酬的苦闷。"无情汴水"两句自是高妙,令人不觉想起李清照语:只恐双溪舴艋舟,载不动,许多愁。

The Beautiful Lady Yu

River Huai's waves seem to beat my pillow till dawn;
A ray of moonbeam peeps at me forlorn.
The heartless River Bian flows eastward down,
Laden with parting grief, you've left the town.

Once we got drunk by riverside bamboo and flower,
My tears made sweet wine sour.
How could a mirror not be stained with dust?
Who could predict the trouble brewing up in gust?

调笑令

渔父,
渔父,
江上微风细雨。
青蓑黄箬①裳衣②,
红酒白鱼暮归。
归暮,
归暮,
长笛一声何处?

> ①箬:箬笠,一种由箬竹的箬叶编成的帽子。
> ②裳(cháng)衣:下身服饰。

  短短三句,描出一幅披风沐雨、载酒归暮的江上渔父形象,本似色泽明丽的渔舟唱晚,却因一声长笛化作恬淡中略带苍凉的水墨归暮图。渔父逍遥自足,闲适自乐,或许正是词人此刻心中所羡?

Song of Flirtation

Fisherman,

Fisherman,

On the river in gentle wind and rain,

In blue straw cloak, broad-brimmed hat on the head,

He comes back late at dusk with fish white and wine red.

Come late with ease,

Come late with ease,

He plays his flute, but who knows where he is?

洞仙歌

仆七岁时,见眉州老尼,姓朱,忘其名,年九十岁。自言尝随其师入蜀主孟昶①宫中。一日大热,蜀主与花蕊夫人②夜纳凉摩诃池上,作一词。朱具能记之。今四十年,朱已死久矣,人无知此词者。但记其首两句。暇日寻味,岂《洞仙歌令》乎?乃为足之云。

冰肌玉骨,
自清凉无汗。
水殿风来暗香满。

① 孟昶(chǎng):五代十国后蜀末代皇帝。
② 花蕊夫人:孟昶的妃子。

苏轼在《洞仙歌》的小序中提到,他七岁时曾听过蜀主孟昶的《洞仙歌令》,但四十年后只记得首两句,于是,苏轼便根据自己的记忆和丰富的想象,补足这首词,再现了五代时期后蜀国君孟昶和他的妃子花蕊夫人夏夜在摩诃池上纳凉的情形。

开篇极言花蕊夫人之美:冰为肌、玉为骨,再配以水、风、香、月之境烘托佳人绰约风姿,赋予她一种超凡脱俗、

Song of a Fairy in the Cave
Madame Pistil

When I was seven, a ninety-year-old nun told me that she had visited the palace of King Meng Chang, where she saw, on a sweltering hot night, the king and his favorite wife Madame Pistil sitting in the shade by a big pool, writing a poem, which she could still recite. Now forty years have passed. As the nun died long ago, nobody knows that poem now. I still remember the first two lines and think it is perhaps written to the tune of the "Song of a Fairy in the Cave". So I complete Meng Chang's poem as follows:

Your jade-like bones and ice-like skin
Are naturally sweatless, fresh and cool.
The breeze brings the unperceivable fragrance in
And fills the bower by the pool.

清冷高洁的气质；下阕由室内转自室外，描绘一幅星河寂寂、凉风习习、爱侣携手、月下徘徊的美好场景。"但屈指、西风几时来，又不道流年，暗中偷换"为点睛之笔，似花蕊夫人自语，又似词人叹息——时光匆匆、岁月无情，如花美眷不过似水流年！全词想象奇特，波澜起伏，空灵清隽，读来令人神往。

绣帘开、一点明月窥人。
人未寝,
欹枕钗横鬓乱。

起来携素手,
庭户无声,
时见疏星渡河汉。
试问夜如何?
夜已三更,
金波③淡、玉绳④低转。
但屈指、西风几时来,
又不道⑤流年,
暗中偷换。

③金波:指月光。
④玉绳:星名,常泛指群星。
⑤不道:不觉。

The embroidered screen rolled up lets in

A bright spot of a moon which peeps at you there

Leaning on the pillow, not asleep, a hairpin

Across your dishevelled hair.

We two rise hand in hand,

Silent in the courtyard we stand.

At times we see shooting stars stray

Across the Milky Way.

How old has night become?

The watchmen thrice have beaten the drum.

The golden moonbeams begin to fade,

Low is the Big Dipper's string of jade.

We count on our fingers when the west wind will blow.

What can we do with years which drift as rivers flow?

洞仙歌·咏柳

江南腊尽,
早梅花开后,
分付①新春与垂柳。
细腰肢、自有入格②风流。
仍更是,
骨体清英雅秀。

永丰坊③那畔,
尽日无人,
谁见金丝④弄晴昼?
断肠是、飞絮时,
绿叶成阴,
无个事、一成⑤消瘦,
又莫是、东风逐君来,
便吹散眉间,
一点春皱。

①分付:付托,寄意。
②格:格调。
③永丰坊:地名,在洛阳。
④金丝:比喻柳树的垂枝。
⑤一成:宋代口语,即"渐渐"。

  体态婀娜、风韵秀雅却境况清寂、无人一顾,词中句句写垂柳,却句句是佳人宛出。拂柳之姿,弱柳之质,为谁弄晴昼?为谁成消瘦?终是令人同情。

Song of a Fairy in the Cave
The Willow Tree

In the end of the year on Southern shore

When early mume blossoms disappear,

The newcome spring dwells on the weeping willow tree,

Its slender waist reveals a personality free,

And what is more,

Its trunk appears more elegant and freer.

Along the way

There are no sight-seers all the day.

Who'd come to see your golden thread in sunlight sway?

Your heart would break to see catkins fly,

Your green leaves make a shade of deep dye.

Having nothing to do,

You would grow thinner, too.

If you come again with vernal breeze now,

It would dispel the vernal grief on your brow.

红梅（三首选一）

怕愁贪睡独开迟，
自恐冰容不入时[1]。
故作小红桃杏色，
尚余孤瘦雪霜姿。
寒心未肯随春态，
酒晕无端上玉肌。
诗老[2]不知梅格[3]在，
更看绿叶与青枝。

[1] 不入时：不合时俗。
[2] 诗老：指北宋诗人石延年。
[3] 格：风格，品格。

这首诗是作者被贬黄州期间，因读北宋诗人石延年《红梅》一诗有感，随即也作了《红梅》三首，此为其一。诗人巧妙地将红梅与佳人融为一体，红梅艳如桃杏却开在寒冷冬季，和那玉肌冰容、傲世独立的佳人岂不相同？而自己呢，才高多舛不入时，岂不也如那红梅"尚余孤瘦雪霜姿"！至此，一个不愿与世俗同流合污、随波逐流的东坡形象尽出。全词托物咏志，梅与佳人、诗人的形象重叠，不失为一首咏物佳作。

Red Mume Blossom

Enjoying sleep and shunning sadness, she blossoms late,
Afraid an icy look might not be up to date.
Like peach and apricot she rouges her fair face;
Like snow and frost she has her lonely, slender grace.
Her heart is cold and will not seek to please as spring;
Her skin like jade is tinged with the hue wine would bring.
How can she be described? An old poet knows not
But says she's leafless peach and green-boughed apricot.

正月二十日与潘、郭二生[1]出郊寻春,忽记去年是日同至女王城[2]作诗,乃和前韵

东风未肯入东门,
走马还寻去岁村。
人似秋鸿来有信,
事如春梦了无痕。
江城白酒三杯酽[3],
野老苍颜一笑温。
已约年年为此会,
故人不用赋招魂。

[1]潘郭二生:苏轼在黄州的朋友潘大临和郭遘。
[2]女王城:即黄州东十五里的永安城。
[3]酽(yàn):指酒的味道醇厚。

作此诗时,苏轼已到黄州两年。还是那个日子,还是那个地方,还是那些人去寻春,感受却不同了。诗人敏感地发现:貌似不变的时空里岁月匆匆,什么都在发生改变,曾经的得意、繁华、欢乐、富贵……都如春梦缥缈散去,人生虚无,也许恰当放下,借此排解心中的苦闷和痛苦!然而放下真有那么容易吗?暂且不管,先告慰故人:我在黄州过得很好,不必为我的处境担忧。即使自己愁闷,也愿安慰他人,展现了作者豁达的胸襟。全诗对仗工整,尤其颔联比喻新颖,把抽象的事物塑造得美妙具体,成为千古名句。

Seeking Spring

Seeking spring with two friends on the 20th day of the 1st lunar month reminded me of the poem written on the same day last year, and I wrote these lines in the same rhymes.

The east wind will not enter the east gate with glee,
I ride to seek the village visited last year.
Old friends still ask autumn swans to bring word to me;
The bygones like spring dreams have left no traces here.
Three cups of strong wine by riverside keep us late;
A smile of the grey-haired countryman warms my heart.
Each year we will meet here on an appointed date,
It's useless for my friends to hasten my depart.

春日

鸣鸠^①乳燕寂无声,
日射西窗泼眼明。
午醉醒来无一事,
只将春睡赏^②春晴。

①鸣鸠：斑鸠。
②赏：犒赏。

  宁静的春日午后，没有声音打扰，明媚的阳光洒在地面，午睡醒来，闲来无事，便尽兴欣赏与享受美好明朗的春天。宁静时光，平常生活，经诗人笔墨，便有种顺其自然、自得其乐的松弛感。

Spring Day

Cooing pigeons and nursling swallows weave no cries,
Sunlight piercing western windows dazzles the eyes.
Awakened from noonday torpor, indolent I stay,
And enjoy in my spring sleep a sunny spring day.

寒食①雨二首

一

自我来黄州,

已过三寒食,

年年欲惜春,

春去不容惜。

今年又苦雨,

两月秋萧瑟,

卧闻海棠花,

泥污燕脂雪②。

暗中偷负去,

夜半真有力。

何殊③病少年,

病起头已白。

①寒食:节日名,在清明节的前一天。
②燕脂雪:指海棠花瓣。
③何殊:何异。

寒食前后阴雨连绵、萧瑟如秋。那受苦雨摧折而凋落陷入污泥的海棠,何等无助与悲惨。此诗写于谪居黄州的第三年,此时的苏轼依然处境艰难,生活凄凉,心情孤郁。借命运相似的海棠表现贬谪之悲和内心的绝望。

Rain at the Cold-food Festival

I

Since I came to Huangzhou, I've passed
Three Cold-food days devot'd to fast.
Each year I wish fair spring to stay,
But spring will go without delay.
This year again we suffer from rains,
For two months dreary autumn reigns.
Lying in bed, I smell crab-apple flowers,
Upon whose rouge and snow mud showers.
The rouge has taken stealthy flight,
Borne away by the Strong at midnight.
The snow is like a sick youth's head
Turning white when he's up from his bed.

二

春江欲入户，
雨势来不已，
小屋如渔舟，
蒙蒙[4]水云里。
空庖[5]煮寒菜，
破灶烧湿苇。
那知是寒食？
但见乌衔纸。
君门深九重，
坟墓在万里。
也拟哭途穷，
死灰吹不起！

[4]蒙蒙：雨迷茫的样子。
[5]庖（páo）：厨房。

II

Spring flood is coming up to my gate,
My small cot looks like a fishing boat.
The pouring rain will not abate,
My cot on misty waves will float.
I cook food in a kitchen in decay
And burn wet reeds in a cracked stove.
Who can tell 'tis the Cold-food day
But for the money-paper burned above?
The royal palace has gate on gate;
My household graves far away lie.
At the road's end I'd lament my fate,
But dead ashes blown up cannot fly.

次荆公①韵

骑驴渺渺入荒陂②,
想见先生未病时。
劝我试求三亩宅,
从公已觉十年迟。

①荆公:指王安石。
②陂(bēi):山坡。

  东坡驴行慢慢,思绪渺渺,想念、遗憾、尊敬各种情绪入怀:当年轰轰烈烈意气风发的荆公王安石已然迟暮病颓,噫!若非政事牵累,半生政敌早为一生之友!今虽泯然一笑,十年光阴岂能追回?!
  东坡拜曰:轼今日野服拜见大丞相!王荆公答:礼法岂为你我而设?!两人相视大笑!送别苏轼时,荆公看着他的背影道:不知更几百年,方有此等人物!
  政坛对搏,是二人之不幸;人生相惜,是中华文化之幸!

Reply to Wang Anshi, Former Prime Minister

Riding an ass, I come from afar to visit you,
Still imagining you as healthy as I knew.
You advise me to buy a house at your next gate,
I'd like to follow you, but it is ten years late.

题①西林②壁

横看成岭侧成峰,
远近高低各不同。
不识庐山真面目,
只缘③身在此山中。

①题：题写。
②西林：西林寺，在江西庐山。
③缘：由于。

苏轼由黄州贬赴汝州时经过九江，游览庐山。瑰丽的山水触发逸兴壮思，于是写下了此诗。它既是游观庐山后的总结：身在庐山之中，看到的只有一峰一岭一丘一壑，局部而已，这必然带有片面性；同时，又借景说理，指出观察问题应客观全面，如果主观片面，就得不出正确的结论。要认识事物的真相与全貌，必须超越狭小的范围，摆脱主观成见。

Written on the Wall at West Forest Temple

It's a range viewed in face and peaks viewed from the side,
Assuming different shapes viewed from far and wide.
Of Mountain Lu we cannot make out the true face,
For we are lost in the heart of the very place.

琴诗

若①言琴上有琴声,
放在匣中何②不鸣?
若言声在指头上,
何不于君指上听?

①若:如果。
②何:为何。

  苏轼听人弹琴后有感而发,用平实晓畅的文字写下此诗。他通过反问,巧妙而形象地说明了是琴与指的结合,才产生了精美的琴声。诗人借琴声解说禅理,揭示了"有"与"无"结合、"有"和"无"的统一,才能生成万物的普遍道理。

Song of the Lute

If you say music from the lute does rise,
Why in its case will not vibrate its string?
If you say the sound in the fingers lies,
Why have we never heard the fingers sing?

南堂①（五首选二）

一

江上西山②半隐堤，
此邦③台馆④一时西。
南堂独有西南向，
卧看千帆落浅溪。

二

扫地焚香闭阁眠，
簟⑤纹如水帐如烟。
客来梦觉知何处？
挂起西窗浪接天。

①南堂：在临皋亭，俯临长江，是作者被贬黄州时的住所。
②西山：即樊山，在今湖北鄂州，是作者被贬黄州时的读书处。
③此邦：指黄州。
④台馆：楼台馆阁。
⑤簟（diàn）：竹席。

元丰六年五月，被贬黄州的苏轼在友人的大力支持下，于临皋亭的南畔筑三间屋，名曰南堂，建成后即景抒怀。诗人在第一首诗中以特写镜头刻画南堂窗含大江，极目远眺的景色：只见江中千帆停泊，江面一片烟波渺茫。淡淡几笔，勾勒出一幅景物寥廓的画面。第二首则写自己打扫、午休的

The Southern Hall

I

The western hills are half hidden by river banks,

All the pavilions of this country face the west.

The Southern Hall has windows on the south and west flanks,

Abed, I see a thousand sails and waves with white crest.

II

Floor swept, incense burning and doors closed, I lie flat

In a mist-like curtain on a ripple-marked mat.

When a guest comes, I wake and wonder where am I,

West windows propp'd open, I see waves meet the sky.

生活日常。清凉如水的竹席和轻柔似烟的纱帐,美丽如梦境。客来被惊醒时,他仍迷离恍惚,不知身处何处。唯见窗外碧浪连接远天、浩渺无边的清远壮阔之景,衬托了诗人超然尘外的闲静心境。

海棠

东风袅袅①泛崇光②,
香雾空蒙月转廊。
只恐夜深花睡去,
故烧高烛照红妆。

①袅袅:微风吹拂的样子。
②崇光:华美的光泽。

这首诗写于宋神宗元丰七年(1084),当时作者被贬黄州已经五个年头。诗人首句用一"泛"字,活化出了春意浓浓,海棠盛开的景象。可惜香气四溢,却无人欣赏。唯有诗人担心"夜深花睡去"。一个"恐"字,不但强调了诗人对海棠的痴情,更暗示了自己的孤寂、冷清。用高烧的红烛,为海棠驱除这长夜的黑暗。"烧""照"两字表面上都写作者对花的喜爱与呵护,其实也不禁流露出些许贬居生活的郁郁寡欢。

Crab-apple Flower

The flower in east wind exhales a tender light
And spreads a fragrant mist when the moon turns away.
I am afraid she'd fall asleep at dead of night;
A candle's lit to make her look fair as by day.

归宜兴留题竹西寺[1]

此生已觉都无事,
今岁仍逢大有年。
山寺归来闻好语,
野花啼鸟亦欣然。

[1] 竹西寺:位于扬州。

此诗描绘了一种超脱世俗、心境宁静的生活状态。诗人似已经看破红尘,对一切俗务都不再放在心上。借助山寺、野花和啼鸟等意象,展现了诗人对自然界的热爱以及追求内心平静的生活态度。

Written in Zhuxi Temple
on My Way Back to Yixing

The crop still bears a plentiful harvest this year,

I feel myself already free from worldly care.

On my way back from the Temple good news I hear,

Even wild flowers and song birds have a cheerful air.

惠崇[1]春江晚景二首

一

竹外桃花三两枝,
春江水暖鸭先知。
蒌蒿[2]满地芦芽[3]短,
正是河豚欲上时。

二

两两归鸿欲破群[4],
依依还似北归人。
遥知朔[5]漠多风雪,
更待江南半月春。

①惠崇：北宋僧人，能诗善画，《春江晚景》是其所作画之名。
②蒌蒿：草名。
③芦芽：芦苇的幼芽。
④破群：离开飞行的队伍。
⑤朔：北方。

　　这两首诗是苏轼题在惠崇所画的《春江晚景》上的。惠崇原画已失，但凭借苏轼形象的语言，再现美妙的意境，甚至画面所不能表现的东西，也通过文字构筑。苏轼以其细致、敏锐的感受，捕捉住季节转换时的景物特征，抒发对早春的喜悦和礼赞之情。

River Scenes on a Spring Evening Written to Accompany Two Pictures Drawn by Monk Huichong

I

Behind bamboo two or three sprays of peach-tree grow,
When spring has warmed the stream, ducks are the first to know.
The land o'verrun by weeds and water studd'd with reeds,
It is time when globefish to swim upstream preceeds.

II

Returning wild geese from the flock would break away,
North-going wayfarers are reluctant to go.
Knowing from afar the desert's still covered with snow,
For half a month more in the South they would fain stay.

南乡子·集句

怅望送春①杯，（杜牧）
渐老逢春能几回？（杜甫）
花满楚城愁远别，（许浑）
伤怀，
何况清丝②急管催？（刘禹锡）

吟断望乡台，（李商隐）
万里归心独上来。（许浑）
景物登临闲始见，（杜牧）
徘徊，
一寸相思一寸灰。（李商隐）

①送春：送别春天。
②清丝：指丝弦乐器。

　　选取前人成句合为一篇叫集句。本词起笔取杜牧诗句点出对酒伤春之情。又拿杜甫伤老一句道出自己的相似心情，看花叹老，对酒思家，愁深似楚城花海。伤怀二字，分量极重。人穷则思返本，何况东坡此时远别故土，为此下片纵笔望乡情切。归心万里，登临览景却因闲始见。只因此身已闲，

Song of Southern Country

Wine cup in hand, I see spring off in vain. (Du Mu)
How many times can I, oldened, see spring again? (Du Fu)
The town in bloom, I'm grieved to be far, far away. (Xu Hun)
Can I be gay?
The pipes and strings do hasten spring not to delay. (Liu Yuxi)

I croon and gaze from Homesick Terrace high; (Li Shangyin)
Coming for miles and miles, alone I mount and sigh. (Xu Hun)
Things can be best enjoyed in a leisurely way; (Du Mu)
For long I stay,
And inch by inch my heart burns into ashes grey. (Li Shangyin)

始得登临见春景，饱醮自身遭贬谪无可作为的莫大痛苦。辗转徘徊，反思内心，正是一寸相思一寸灰。集句为词，信手拈来，浑然天成，可见东坡的博学强识及思想的灵活自由。

京都

一朵红云捧玉皇

水龙吟·次韵①章质夫②杨花词

似花还似非花,
也无人惜从教③坠。
抛家傍路,
思量却是,
无情有思。
萦损柔肠,
困酣④娇眼,
欲开还闭。
梦随风万里,
寻郎去处,
又还被、莺呼起。

①次韵:用原作之韵,并按照原作用韵次序进行创作,称为次韵。
②章质夫:即章楶(jié),北宋名将、诗人。
③从教:任凭。
④困酣:困倦至极。

  这首词用象征、隐喻,将杨花与思妇紧密糅合在一起,句句写杨花又句句是写思妇,既绘形,又传神。既表现思妇青春已逝、情人不归的幽怨,又抒发自己怜春、惜春的深情,更在词中融入自己宦海浮沉的感慨和对于时事的惆怅,抒情浓郁,意蕴丰富,韵味深长。表面婉约,内里沉郁。整首词极擅化用典故,写得舒卷自如,圆润顺畅,笔墨空灵洒脱,毫无束缚之感。

Water Dragon's Chant
Willow Catkins

After Zhang Zhifu's lyric on willow catkins, using the same rhyming words.

They seem to be and not to be flowers,
None pity them when they fall in showers.
Deserting home,
By the roadside they roam;
I think they have no feeling to impart,
But they must have thoughts deep.
Grief numbs their tender heart,
Their wistful eyes heavy with sleep,
About to open, yet closed again.
They dream of going with the wind for long,
Long miles to find a tender-hearted man,
But are aroused by the orioles' song.

不恨此花飞尽,
恨西园、落红难缀⑤。
晓来雨过,
遗踪何在?
一池萍碎。
春色三分,
二分尘土,
一分流水。
细看来,
不是杨花点点,
是离人泪。

⑤缀:连结。

I do not grieve willow catkins have flown away,

But that in Western Garden the fallen red

Cannot be gathered. When dawns the day

And rain is o'er, we cannot find their traces

But a pond with broken duckweeds o'erspread.

Of spring's three graces,

Two have gone with the roadside dust,

And one with the waves. If you just

Take a close look, you will never

Find catkins but tears of those who sever,

Which drop by drop

Fall without stop.

贺新郎

乳燕飞华屋。
悄无人、桐阴转午。
晚凉新浴。
手弄生绡①白团扇②,
扇手一时似玉。
渐困倚、孤眠清熟③。
帘外谁来推绣户?
枉教人、梦断瑶台曲。
又却是,
风敲竹。

①生绡(xiāo):丝绢。
②团扇:汉班婕妤《团扇诗》:"新裂齐纨素,鲜洁如霜雪。裁为合欢扇,团团似明月。"后常以喻指佳人失宠。
③清熟:谓睡眠安稳。

这首词运用比兴手法,以秾艳孤高、不与浮花浪蕊争艳的石榴花象征佳人,又借佳人迟暮,寄托自己怀才不遇、孤高自守的政治情怀。构思巧妙,笔墨宛曲,托意高远。全篇运用映衬烘托、象征暗示手法颇为细致。如:用乳燕飞、桐阴转、风敲竹烘托清幽洁净的庭院环境,又借以映衬佳人的孤独寂寞。以扇手似玉表现佳人的纯洁玲珑,并暗示她秋后

Congratulations to the Bridegroom The Beauty and the Pomegranate Flower

Young swallows fly along the painted eave,

Which none perceive.

The shade of plane trees keeps away

The hot noonday

And brings an evening fresh and cool

For the bathing lady beautiful.

She flirts a round fan of silk made,

Both fan and hand as white as jade.

Tired by and by,

She falls asleep with lonely sigh.

Who's knocking at the curtained door

团扇似的命运。以孤眠、梦断透露她对理想的憧憬、追求、失望和惆怅的复杂心态,细致入微。特别是以石榴花象征佳人,既写出花形花态,花格花品,又使之与佳人和合为一,使人读来平添了许多意趣。整首词与一般的婉丽之作不同,它用华艳的形象与缠绵的格调写政治题材,富有独创性。

石榴半吐红巾蹙④。
待浮花、浪蕊都尽,
伴君幽独。
秾艳⑤一枝细看取,
芳心千重似束。
又恐被、秋风惊绿。
若待得君来向此,
花前对酒不忍触。
共粉泪,
两簌簌⑥。

④红巾蹙(cù):形容石榴花半开时如红巾皱缩。蹙,皱。
⑤秾(nóng)艳:色彩艳丽。
⑥簌簌:纷纷落下的样子。

That she can dream sweet dreams no more?

It's again the breeze who

Is swaying green bamboo.

The pomegranate flower opens half her lips

Which look like wrinkled crimson strips;

When all the wanton flowers fade,

Alone she'll be the beauty's maid.

How charming is her blooming branch, behold!

Her fragrant heart seems wrapped a thousand fold.

But she's afraid to be surprised by western breeze

Which withers all the green leaves on the trees.

The beauty comes to drink to the flower fair;

To see her withered too she cannot bear.

Then tears and flowers

Would fall in showers.

鹊桥仙·七夕送陈令举①

缑山②仙子，
高情云渺，
不学痴牛骏女③。
凤箫声断月明中，
举手谢、时人欲去。

客槎④曾犯，
银河波浪，
尚带天风海雨。
相逢一醉是前缘，
风雨散、飘然何处？

① 陈令举：陈舜俞，字令举，苏轼的好友。
② 缑（gōu）山：在今河南省洛阳市偃师区。
③ 痴牛骏（ái）女：指牛郎织女。
④ 槎（chá）：竹筏。

此词借七夕下笔，不写男女离恨，而咏送别朋友的情意，别有一番新味。借用王子乔飘然仙去的故事，称颂一种超尘拔俗、不被柔情羁绊的飘逸旷放襟怀，以开解友人的离思别苦。"一醉是前缘"，含慰藉之意；"飘然何处"，蕴感慨无限。

Immortal at the Magpie Bridge
Farewell on Double Seventh Eve

Like the immortal leaving the crowd,

Wafting above the cloud,

Unlike the Cowherd and the Maid who fond remain,

You blow your flute in moonlight,

Waving your hand, you go in flight.

Your boat will go away

Across the Milky Way,

In celestial wind and rain.

We've met and drunk as if by fate.

Where will you waft when wind and rain abate?

八声甘州·寄参寥子①

有情风、万里卷潮来,
无情送潮归。
问钱塘江上,
西兴②浦口,
几度斜晖?
不用思量今古,
俯仰昔人非。
谁似东坡老,
白首忘机③?

① 参寥子:即僧人道潜,字参寥。善诗,与苏轼是诗友。
② 西兴:即西陵,在今杭州市萧山区之西。
③ 忘机:忘掉世俗的心机。

这首词上片借钱塘江潮和西兴斜晖渲染离情,引出对古今变迁、人事代谢的感慨,并以超尘拔俗、泰然从容的态度面对这一切的变更。下片写西湖春景,回顾与参寥在杭一同游赏的情景和相知相得的友谊,表明自己超然物外、寄情山

Eight Beats of Ganzhou Song
For a Buddhist Friend

The heart-stirring breeze brings in the tidal bore;

The heartless wind sees it flow out from river shore.

At the river's mouth

Or the ferry south,

How many times have we heard parting chimes?

Don't grieve over the past!

The world changes fast.

Who could be like me,

Though white-haired, yet carefree?

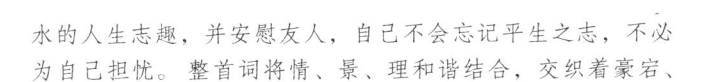

水的人生志趣，并安慰友人，自己不会忘记平生之志，不必为自己担忧。整首词将情、景、理和谐结合，交织着豪宕、闲逸、超旷的复杂情绪，云锦成章，天衣无缝。

记取西湖西畔,
正春山好处,
空翠烟霏。
算诗人相得④,
如我与君稀。
约他年、东还海道,
愿谢公⑤、雅志⑥莫相违。
西州路,
不应回首,
为我沾衣。

④相得:相投合。
⑤谢公:指谢安。
⑥雅志:很早立下的志愿。

Do not forsake the western shore of the lake:

On fine day the vernal hills are green;

On rainy day they are veiled by misty screen.

Few poets would be

Such bosom friends as you and me.

Do not forget in our old age,

We'll live together in hermitage.

Even if I should disappear,

You should not turn to weep for your compeer.

临江仙·送钱穆父[①]

一别都门[②]三改火[③],
天涯踏尽红尘。
依然一笑作春温。
无波真古井[④],
有节是秋筠[⑤]。

惆怅孤帆连夜发,
送行淡月微云。
尊前不用翠眉[⑥]颦[⑦]。
人生如逆旅[⑧],
我亦是行人。

①钱穆:钱勰,字穆父,苏轼的好友。
②都门:都城的城门。此借指都城汴京。
③改火:古代钻木取火,四季使用不同的木材,称为"改火",此处指年度的更替。
④古井:枯井。比喻内心沉静,不为外界所动。
⑤筠(yún):竹子的皮,此处代指竹子。
⑥翠眉:古代妇女的一种眉饰。
⑦颦:皱眉。
⑧逆旅:旅店。

这首词一改以往送别词缠绵感伤、哀怨愁苦或慷慨悲凉的格调,创新意于法度之中,寄妙理于豪放之外,议论风生,直抒性情,写得既有情韵,又富理趣。上片写久别重逢,"无波"两句赞友人能以道自守,保持耿介风节,其实也正是作

Riverside Daffodils
Farewell to a Friend

Three years have passed since we left the capital;
We've trodden all the way from rise to fall.
Still I smile as on warm spring day.
In ancient well no waves are raised;
Upright, the autumn bamboo's praised.

Melancholy, your lonely sail departs at night;
Only a pale cloud sees you off in pale moonlight.
You need no songstress to drink your sorrow away.
Life is like a journey;
I too am on my way.

者坚持正直操守，又能以一种恬淡自安来对待世事纷争的人生态度的高度概括。下片写月夜送别，"人生"两句以极平易的语言劝慰友人忘却升沉得失，表现出超然物外、随遇而安的旷达、洒脱情怀。

书李世南[①]所画秋景（二首选一）

野水参差落涨痕，
疏林欹倒出霜根。
扁舟一棹归何处？
家在江南黄叶村。

[①]李世南：宋代著名画家。

    这首题画诗前两句描绘荒野秋景，给读者展示的是一幅萧疏的水乡深秋景物图。后两句发挥想象，于景物中融入人情，赋予画面悠然无尽的情思，表达了诗人对江村生活的羡慕向往，同时也流露出诗人厌烦市朝、向往自然的情趣。

Autumn Scene Written to Accompany a Picture Drawn by Li Shinan

Creeks crisscross the meadow, banks scarred where water rose;
Sparse trees slant and let their frost-bitten roots stick out.
Do you know where the single-oared, leaf-like boat goes?
To the village of yellow leaves or thereabout.

书鄢陵①王主簿②所画折枝③二首

一

论画以形似,
见与儿童邻。
赋诗必此诗,
定非知诗人。
诗画本一律,
天工与清新。
边鸾雀写生,
赵昌花传神。
何如此两幅,
疏淡含精匀!
谁言一点红,
解寄无边春!

①鄢陵:即今河南省鄢陵县。
②王主簿:生平不可考。主簿,官职名。
③折枝,花卉画的一种表现手法,花卉不画全株,只画连枝折下来的部分,故名折枝。

这组题画诗通过对王主簿所画折枝花的高度评价,提出了关于诗歌与绘画的精辟艺术见解。首先,作者反对片面追求"形似",认为诗、画都应形神结合,意在传神。其次,他指出诗画虽各有其艺术特点,但在基本的艺术规律上却是共同的,都要巧夺天工,清新自然。在写法上,通篇几乎全用议论,但能将哲理融于情景之中。

Flowering Branches Written on Paintings by Secretary Wang of Yanling

I

To overstress resemblance of form

In painting is a childish view.

Who thinks in verse there is a norm,

To poetry he's got no clew.

In painting as in poetry,

We like what's natural and new.

Bian Luan painted birds vividly;

Zhao Chang's flowers to nature were true.

But these two pictures surpass them:

They're fairer and more elaborate.

We won't believe from a red stem

The beauty of spring can radiate.

二

瘦竹如幽人，
幽花如处女。
低昂枝上雀，
摇荡花间雨。
双翎决将起，
众叶纷自举。
可怜采花蜂，
清蜜寄两股。
若人富天巧，
春色入毫楮④。
悬知⑤君能诗，
寄声求妙语。

④毫楮（chǔ）：毛笔和纸。
⑤悬知：猜想。

II

Slender bamboos look like recluse;

Like maidens blossom lonely flowers.

Birds bend the branch which they let loose,

And shaken flowers fall in showers.

They flap their wings and up they fly

And stir all the leaves of the trees.

With nectar gathered on the thigh,

Busy are the laborious bees.

This painter has a gift for art,

His brush preserves the beauty of spring.

I think he is a poet at heart,

And wait for a reply this verse will bring.

赠刘景文[1]

荷尽已无擎[2]雨盖,
菊残犹有傲霜枝。
一年好景君须[3]记,
最是橙黄橘绿时。

[1] 刘景文:即刘季孙,北宋诗人,苏轼称其为"慷慨奇士"。
[2] 擎:举。
[3] 须:应当,需要。

    这首小诗借荷、菊、橙、橘四种时物的变化特征,表现深秋初冬江南的景色,写得色彩明丽,风骨遒劲,生机勃勃。诗人借物喻人,赞颂刘景文斗风傲霜的品格与节操;又托物抒情,含蓄地抒发自己旷达开朗、不同凡俗的性情和胸襟;更即景寓理,暗示时间和人生的宝贵,启示人们要珍惜美好年华。整首诗情、景、理交融。

To Liu Jingwen

Lotuses put up no umbrellas to the rain;

Yet frost-proof branches of chrysanthemum remain.

Do not forget of a year the loveliest scene:

When oranges are yellow and tangerines are green.

上元^①侍饮^②楼上三首呈同列（三首选一）

澹月疏星绕建章^③，
仙风吹下御炉香。
侍臣鹄立^④通明殿，
一朵红云^⑤捧玉皇^⑥。

①上元：元宵节。
②侍饮：臣子赴皇帝的宴会。
③建章：建章宫。
④鹄（hú）立：像天鹅一样引颈直立。
⑤红云：比喻穿红袍的臣子。
⑥玉皇：指宋朝皇帝。

　　此诗写苏轼在元宵佳节，参加宋哲宗主持的宴会情形。澹月疏星中，巍峨的皇宫高耸入云，仙境吹来的风合着香味，宁静庄严。侍臣们像天鹅般伸长脖子，盼望皇帝的到来。红云簇拥，如神仙出行。哇，皇帝尊严！歌功颂德的此诗，让我们领略到宋代皇帝宴请群臣时，仍然保持着庄严肃穆、典雅隆重的气氛。

Royal Banquet on Lantern Festival

The morning moon and stars shed light on palace hall;
Celestial breeze spreads royal incense over all.
The ministers attend the banquet like cranes proud,
The emperor seems to reign from the rosy cloud.

儋州

此生归路愈茫然

慈湖夹[1]阻风（五首选三）

一

捍索[2]桅竿立啸空，
篙师酣寝浪花中。
故应菅蒯[3]知心腹，
弱缆能争万里风。

①慈湖夹：在今安徽省当涂县北。
②捍索：桅杆两边的绳索。船行驶时下垂，停泊时用以揽船。
③菅（jiān）蒯（kuǎi）：茅草之类，可编绳索。

二

此生归路愈茫然，
无数青山水拍天。
犹有小船来卖饼，
喜闻墟落在山前。

绍圣元年，六道贬谪之令促东坡一路向南，去往惠州。贬途遇大风阻隔，亦是仕途遇风波。人生茫然，然徜徉山水，放舟江湖，有小船卖饼、有墟市可逛，仍见其坦然与从容！

东坡喜欢墟市的热闹与烟火气，幼时即与子由"年年废书走市观"，如今六旬翁即便身在人生茫然的贬谪之途，也能见墟市便喜，一笑！

Held up by Head Winds on the Gorge of the Kind Lake

I

The mast with stretched ropes stands sighing in the air,
The punter soundly sleeps by the white-crested waves.
You should repose your trust in these hemp ropes, howe'er:
Weak as they seem, they can stand a strong wind which raves.

II

When can I come back to my hometown? I'm at a loss.
Beyond countless blue hills waves rise into the sky.
As cakes are sold in a small boat we come across,
We are glad to find there is a village nearby.

三

卧看落月横千丈,
起唤清风得半帆。
且并水村欹侧过,
人间何处不巉岩④!

④巉(chán)岩:山石险峻。这里借喻人生道路上的难行。

III

Abed, I see the setting moon shine far and wide;

Rising, I call the wind and it fills half the sail.

Let us go round the village by the waterside.

How can we in our life encounter no adverse gale?

纵笔

白头萧散①满霜风②,
小阁藤床寄病容。
报道③先生④春睡美,
道人轻打五更钟。

①萧散：萧疏冷落的样子。这里形容头发稀少。
②霜风：形容头发披散的样子。
③报道：报告说。
④先生：作者自指。

岭南风光好，白头病容亦无愁。怕扰春睡美，道人轻敲钟。

诗成于谪岭南第三年，烟瘴之地未曾挫折东坡的意志，种药、施药、行医、修桥、筑路，东坡"不辞长做岭南人"了，白鹤峰新居成，骨肉相聚，东坡准备终老于此，是以乐而生欢，由欢而成诗。

然诗成了，贬谪诏令亦至，只因"春睡美"惹宵小怨憎恼怒，东坡再度被贬至天涯海角的儋州。人的恶在故意打碎人的美好情感那一刻，最是触及人性的底线！

An Impromptu Verse Written in Exile

Dishevelled white hair flows in the wind like frost spread,
In my small study I lie ill in a wicker bed.
Knowing that I am sleeping a sweet sleep in spring,
The Taoist priest takes care morning bells softly ring.

被酒①独行,遍至子云、威、徽、先觉四黎②之舍(三首选二)

一

半醒半醉问③诸黎,
竹刺藤梢步步迷。
但寻牛矢④觅归路,
家在牛栏西复西。

二

总角⑤黎家三小童,
口吹葱叶⑥送迎翁。
莫作天涯万里意,
溪边自有舞雩⑦风⑧。

① 被酒:带有醉意,刚喝过酒。
② 四黎:子云、威、徽、先觉都是海南黎族人,姓黎,故称"四黎"。
③ 问:拜访,访问。
④ 牛矢:牛粪。
⑤ 总角:古时儿童男未及冠,女未及笄时的发型。头发梳成两个发髻,如头顶两角,借指幼年。
⑥ 口吹葱叶:一种儿童游戏。
⑦ 舞雩(yú):古代求雨时举行的伴有乐舞的祭祀。
⑧ 风:民风。

  题目即引人捧腹,薄酒微醉,不识归路,拄着竹杖遍访诸邻,方循着牛矢归家。东坡恃大才,惯以俗物入诗,前有蜘蛛、蚯蚓,现有牛矢,怪道东坡虽被称坡仙,却是地仙。

  贬谪至华夏最南端,蛮荒之地早成终老之所,种药施诊教学著书,已然海南民也。如今离岛归中原,父老友邻伤离别,告慰父老:虽相隔万里,然在溪边求雨坛下吹着凉风时,天涯亦若比邻。

Drunken, I Walk Alone to Visit the Four Lis

I

Half drunk, half sober, I ask my way to the four Lis,
Bamboo spikes and rattan creepers tangle before me.
I can but follow the way where cow turds are spread,
And find their houses farther west of cattle shed.

II

Three or four children of the Lis with their hair tressed,
Blowing green onion pipes, welcome me the old guest.
Do not seek happiness to the end of the earth!
By the side of the brook you'll find genuine mirth.

《论语》载，孔子与众弟子言其志，曾点对曰："莫（暮）春者，春服既成，冠者五六人，童子六七人，浴乎沂，风乎舞雩，咏而归。"东坡此时贬谪至天涯海角，远离庙堂，庶几有"风乎舞雩"之乐趣。

纵笔（三首选一）

寂寂东坡一病翁，
白须萧散满霜风。
小儿①误喜朱颜在，
一笑那知是酒红！

① 小儿：指作者第三子苏过。

诗成于元符二年，东坡贬谪至儋州，正值"食无肉、病无药、居无室、出无友、冬无炭、夏无寒泉"之时，实是困窘孤寂抱病之白发翁。幼子苏过夸东坡气色好，东坡暗笑小儿不知是酒红。其实苏过未必不知，故作喜态，果然引东坡一笑。全诗白描，语句平淡却引人情绪跌宕，父子超然旷达恬淡自适之景尽显！

东坡岭南时期《纵笔》诗中有"白头消散满霜风"句，也因此诗被贬至海南，如今续用此句，可见坡公犟骨，虽老而不收，呵呵！

An Impromptu Verse Written by the Seaside

The lonely Master of Eastern Slope lies ill in bed,
Dishevelled white hair flows in the wind like frost spread.
Seeing my crimson face, my son is glad I'm fine,
I laugh for he does not know that I have drunk wine.

澄迈驿①通潮阁②二首

一

倦客愁闻归路遥，
眼明飞阁俯长桥。
贪观③白鹭横秋浦，
不觉青林没晚潮。

二

余生欲老海南村，
帝④遣巫阳⑤招我魂。
杳杳⑥天低鹘没处，
青山一发是中原。

①澄迈驿：设在澄迈县(今海南省北部)的驿站。
②通潮阁：在澄迈县西。
③贪观：久久地看。
④帝：天帝。
⑤巫阳：古代女巫名。
⑥杳杳：无声无影。

其一：倦、愁二字点出天涯贬客归途心境，然眼前飞阁凌空而出，登临阁上，辽远的空中白鹭横江，晚潮初涨，心怀大畅。诗人笔下诗境如画境，一幅空阔辽远的山水画如在眼前。

其二：本以为将终老海南，如今朝廷召回，远望中原不可见，天边飞鹊与青山若隐若现，那里是故乡了吧！

贬谪至儋州，北归之心虽沉却不死，元符三年遇赦，沉寂的归心被重新拨起，虽归途茫茫前路苍苍，然笔下洒脱飘逸，直抒胸怀，笔墨淡然中蕴炽热之情！

The Tide Pavilion at Chengmai Post

I

A tired wayfarer's sad his home is far away,
Seeing a pavilion o'er a bridge on his way.
I admire white egrets crossing autumn riverside,
Unaware the green woods are drowned in evening tide.

II

I'd end my life in the village by the South Sea,
The Celestial Court sends a witch to recall me.
Far, far away birds vanish into the low skies,
Beyond a stretch of blue hills the Central Plain lies.

过岭

七年来往我何堪！
又试曹溪①一勺甘。
梦里似曾迁海外，
醉中不觉到江南。
波生濯足鸣空涧，
雾绕征衣滴翠岚。
谁遣山鸡忽惊起，
半岩花雨落毵毵②。

①曹溪：在广东省曲江东南。
②毵毵（sān）：毛羽细长，此处用来形容毛毛细雨。

　　两过大庾岭，心境大不同，再饮曹溪甘泉，只觉贬谪如梦、北归如醉。碧波浣足，雾气湿衣，山涧流水、濯足水声惊飞山鸡，花落如雨！

　　七年远谪，诗人漫笔调侃，似乎愁绪既已随纸墨晕染，提笔则无忧矣，可见东坡胸中澄澈！曹溪为六祖慧能传法处，东坡提及曹溪，心境应有佛老超然之意。故而下半首笔锋大转，写就一幅山鸡惊飞拍打花枝的生动趣景，然这是山林间日日可见之景，于东坡却是久违！此景让诗人忘却羁旅愁绪，却让读者心有戚戚！

Passing the Ridge

How could I bear journeys to and fro for seven years!
Again I taste sweet water in the Crooked Stream.
With drunken eyes I see the Southern land appears;
My exile by the seaside seems but like a dream.
Waves roaring in the gully can still wash my feet;
Mist dripping like green drops moistens a wayfarer's frock.
As I pass by, a pheasant startled flies so fleet
That flowers fall in showers over half the rock.

归朝欢·和苏坚伯固

我梦扁舟浮震泽①,
雪浪摇空千顷白。
觉来满眼是庐山,
倚天无数开青壁。
此生长接淅②,
与君同是江南客。
梦中游,
觉来清赏,
同作飞梭掷。

① 震泽:太湖。
② 接淅:匆匆忙忙。

　　震泽、雪浪摇空、千顷、满眼庐山、倚天青壁,皆雄奇壮阔之景,诗人扁舟一叶,于此壮阔中从容自适!然下句笔锋急转,"接淅"、"江南客"点明诗人与友人皆宦海漂泊之身,相聚短暂有如飞梭一掷!前文的壮美江山,在此后却是阻隔两人的千山万水!

Happy Return to the Court
In Reply to Su Jian

I dream my leaflike boat on the vast lake afloat,

Snowlike waves surge up for miles and whiten the air.

I wake to find Mount Lu resplendent to my eye,

Blue cliffs upon blue cliffs open against the sky.

I've suffered setbacks all my life long;

You and I sing alike the roamer's song.

Dreaming of boating on the lake,

I like the thrilling scene when awake,

And feel as happy as the shuttle flies.

　　东坡胸襟浩然，贬谪途中与老友暮年相别，笔下依旧气势雄健，疏阔爽朗。东坡曾云词中前四句"盖实梦也"！一叹！

儋州：此生归路愈茫然

明日西风还挂席③,
唱我新词泪沾臆④。
灵均⑤去后楚山空,
澧阳⑥兰芷无颜色。
君才如梦得⑦,
武陵⑧更在西南极。
《竹枝词》,
莫摇⑨新唱,
谁谓古今隔?

③挂席:犹挂帆。
④臆:胸前。
⑤灵均:屈原的字。
⑥澧阳:今湖南省澧县。
⑦梦得:唐代诗人刘禹锡,字梦得。
⑧武陵:今湖南省常德市一带。
⑨莫摇:少数民族名称。

You will set sail in western breeze tomorrow;

I'll croon in tears for you a new verse full of sorrow.

When Poet Qu is gone, the Southern Mountain's bare.

Sweet orchids and clovers will lose their hue

Like the poet of Willow Branch Song, you

Will go farther southwest.

But you may compose as a guest.

And then who says

The modern age cannot surpass the bygone days?

蝶恋花·春景

花褪残红青杏小。
燕子飞时,
绿水人家绕。
枝上柳绵①吹又少。
天涯何处无芳草!

墙里秋千墙外道。
墙外行人,
墙里佳人笑。
笑渐不闻声渐悄。
多情②却被无情③恼。

①柳绵:柳絮。
②多情:此处代指墙外的行人。
③无情:此处代指墙内的佳人。

　　东坡婉约词中,此首庶几最佳。花、青杏、燕子、绿水、柳绵、芳草写就暮春之景,春去也,却非伤春。"青杏小"三字妙绝,引人入胜。墙里、墙外、佳人、行人、多情、无情,多重对比,轻快婉丽,说"恼"却何曾是恼,分明是妙景生妙思,直让人会心一笑!

Butterfly in Love with Flower
Red Flowers Fade

Red flowers fade and green apricots are still small

When swallows pass

Over blue water which surrounds the garden wall.

Most willow catkins have been blown away, alas!

But there is no place where will not grow sweet green grass.

Without the wall there's a path within there's a swing.

A passer-by

Hears the fair maiden's laughter in the garden ring.

As the ringing laughter dies away by and by,

For the enchantress the enchant'd can only sigh.

然《离骚》有"何所独无芳草兮,尔何怀乎故宇"。朝云以东坡比屈原,唱至"天涯何处无芳草"句时泪满衣襟,对东坡暮年仍旧贬谪天涯不得申"致君尧舜"之志、不得回归故里满心哀伤;朝云离世,东坡亦不复再唱此词。小女子怜惜大文豪,深也彻也!大文豪失去小女子,伤也痛也!

西江月·梅花

玉骨①那愁瘴雾②?
冰姿③自有仙风。
海仙时遣探芳丛,
倒挂绿毛幺凤④。

素面常嫌粉涴⑤,
洗妆不褪唇红⑥。
高情已逐晓云空,
不与梨花同梦。

①玉骨:梅花枝干的美称。
②瘴雾:犹瘴气,南方山林中的湿热之气。
③冰姿:淡雅的姿态。
④绿毛幺凤:岭南的一种珍禽,似鹦鹉。
⑤涴(wò):沾污。
⑥唇红:比喻红梅。

    岭梅玉骨冰姿,不惧瘴雾,引得海上仙人遣使者来探,这使者被梅花倾倒,倒挂枝条赏梅,有趣生动。岭梅素花红萼,似美人天然的淡妆红唇。是花是人,是梅花亦是朝云。梅花高洁,朝云高情,从此只恋梅花,不梦梨花。

    此词成于绍圣三年冬,名为咏梅,实悼朝云。六旬翁万里投荒,早已锻就钢筋铁骨,然柔肠千转仍是血肉之躯!朝云在东坡人生之寒冬万里相伴,有若梅花凌寒,然仙姿玉骨却伤于瘴雾,悲乎!

The Moon on the West River
To the Fairy of Mume Flower

Your bones of jade defy miasmal death;

Your flesh of snow exhales immortal breath.

The sea sprite among flowers often sends to you

A golden-eyed, green-feathered cockatoo.

Powder would spoil your face;

Your lips need no rouge cream.

As high as morning cloud you rise with grace;

With pear flower you won't share your dream.